N.D. Gomes graduated from the University of Stirling with a BA in Media & Journalism Studies, and went on to receive her Master's degree in Education in the US. She currently works in a public school system to increase educational opportunities for students with special needs. Previously, N.D. Gomes wrote for the London-based online student political magazine, *deAlign* and stage-managed student plays at the Lee Strasberg Theatre Institute in New York City where she attended for two years.

She currently divides her time between the US and Scotland, but hopes to spend more time at her cottage in Hay-on-Wye in Wales.

Dear Charlie is her debut novel.

DEAR CHARLIE

N.D GOMES

ONE PLACE. MANY STORIES

HQ

An imprint of HarperCollinsPublishers Ltd.
1 London Bridge Street
London SE1 9GF
This paperback edition 2016

1

First published in Great Britain by
HQ, an imprint of HarperCollinsPublishers Ltd. 2016

ISBN: 978-0-00-818116-1
eBook ISBN: 978-0-00-819412-3

Printed and bound by
CPI Group (UK) Ltd, Croydon, CR0 4YY

To my family and Nick for their endless support

Chapter 1

Dear Charlie,

I'm sorry it's taken me seven weeks to write this. Honestly, I still don't know why I am. It's not like you will ever get to read it. It's not like you will ever know how I am feeling. I can't change anything, certainly not the past couple of months. And no matter how hard I try, I can't forget. I'll never be able to forget.

The strange thing is, I can't stop thinking about the small things, like what I had for breakfast that morning, what music I listened to on the radio while I ate, why I chose blue jeans over black cords. But that's just it. These thoughts fill my head all day, but when I open my mouth to share them, I can't. I just can't.

My therapist says if I can't talk about it then maybe writing in a journal will help me. Like

I'm the one who needs help in this family. Yes, I am seeing a therapist. That's how bad things have got around here.

I don't even know where to start. Everything's changed. Mum flits between total denial and hysterics, almost on a daily basis. One minute she acts like she really believes you're just upstairs doing your homework or listening to music, and the next minute it's a complete emotional breakdown all over again. She relives your death every day. My therapist says this is normal, but I'm beginning to question whether there really is a criterion for measuring normality in this kind of a situation.

Dad remains a total enigma as usual, occasionally ranting and pointing fingers. But most of the time he doesn't say anything, for days sometimes. I don't know what is happening in his head, but then again we never did. We do seem to have one thing in common - we both haven't cried, not one tear. I don't see the point. Tears won't reverse your actions, or bring you back. Tears won't let me forget, even if that was possible.

You don't have to look far for Dad now. He's either sitting in front of the TV or has locked himself in the garage, but I don't blame him. I don't go outside much myself. We're famous now, just like you always wanted. Our pictures are always in the newspapers, even our house. They keep using the same photo of you. It's your yearbook picture from last year, the one where you let your hair grow out for it. Mum was so mad at you. She said you didn't look like yourself, which is funny now because obviously we didn't know you at all.

Your room is the same as you left it. Or at least, we think so. The police conducted a search of your bedroom not long after. Mum tried to put the pieces back together. She's always trying. I wasn't much help. I hadn't been in your room in weeks, maybe even months. Either you stopped inviting me in, or I stopped asking to come in. Honestly, I don't remember.

A pair of your shoes is still sitting by the door, next to mine. I see them every time I walk past the door, which I do more often now. I like to look out the window and see the photographers waiting for us beyond the garden. I hide behind the lace curtain, but they probably know I'm there. Occasionally I'll see neighbours walk by, but they usually cross the street to avoid passing our house. Perhaps they think it's a disease that they might catch - a contagious need for death and disorder. Maybe they think I have it too. Maybe I do.

I can't fathom a bigger emotional mess for

someone to have left behind. I wonder if you knew that this would happen. I wonder if you thought about anything at all before you walked into that assembly hall at 8.22am on the last day of school.

Pembrook Academy is still closed. I read in the newspaper on Tuesday that the assembly hall will be torn down and replaced with a memorial garden. The remainder of the school will re-open to students by Christmas. But I won't be there to watch the thick yellow tape being cut by the new headteacher.

They hired a woman this time, and I bet she's not as strict as Mr Healey. I still remember that time you pulled the fire alarms in the building and set off the sprinkler system. It went down as the best prank in history – in the 1994 yearbook anyway. You were suspended for five days around the time that I had the flu. I always thought that you did it only so you could spend those five days with me, playing <u>Doom</u> on Dad's PC and prank-calling strangers from the phonebook – Mr Dungworth, Mrs Shufflebottom. My sides ache just thinking about that. I never laughed so hard. I never did thank you for that.

Thinking about it, I don't remember a time that you ever got sick. You were always the strong one in the family. You worked weekends in the Spar when Dad got laid off, you stood up to him when he got drunk and shouted at Mum, and you put a plaster on my cuts and gave me a slap on the back whenever I came home with a bleeding knee. I don't know who's going to be the strong one now.

Whenever I think about the future, I get a pain in my chest that won't go away. It sucks the breath out of my lungs and makes me feel like I'm drowning in a big swimming pool where no one can see me. So, most of the time I try not to think about the future – that's what Dr Albreck told me to do. She said, 'Focus on the now, Sam. The future can wait,' which actually contradicts what my guidance advisor used to tell us in the university prep classes. Regardless, I'm going to try it Dr Albreck's way. But that doesn't mean that I agree with going to therapy.

What else is new? The new headteacher is called Sheila Bevins. I only know that because I opened a letter that she sent to Mum and Dad. In it she said, 'It would be in the best interest of the students and their families that your son Samuel Macmillan not return to Pembrook Academy. Although we are sensitive to your loss, we feel it best to move forward with a fresh start and not be reminded of the past.'

I didn't realise that my existence was a reminder of the past. I don't even care. I laughed when I first read it, as if my absence from the halls could erase what happened. Nothing will erase what happened. When students return to Pembrook, they might not see the blood on the walls but it's still there and always will be. They're idiots for thinking that they can forget. I don't need to be there to remind them, there are enough shadows to darken the halls of that school regardless of whether I am there or not.

It's a shame too, because I was really getting good at making friends. I even got an invite to Jackson's party last weekend, well technically Geoff did but I was going to go with him. It was cancelled, of course. And, I was planning on asking Sarah Reynolds to go to the cinema with me to see Mission: Impossible, although I doubt she would have said yes. She's a year older and was supposed to be going to Edinburgh University in September, but I don't know if she'll go now. Plus she probably would have wanted to watch Flipper or something.

You missed my birthday. You and I were meant to see the sequel to The Crow. You were obsessed with the first one. It's in the cinema right now, but I don't think I'll ever be able to watch it. Not now, not ever. Why would you make plans with me if you never intended to keep them?

I saw Sarah Reynolds at the funeral - we had just one for all those who died that day. She was wearing a dark navy dress with shoes that made her look taller than she is. Her face was red and blotchy, like the others. I wanted to wave, but I didn't think she would want to see me. I read in the newspaper the following day that over five hundred people showed up for the funeral. I didn't even know we had five hundred people in this small town. I wish I could have stood with them but I watched from a distance. I rested my bike beside a large oak tree and watched from behind it.

I shouldn't have been there, I was asked not to go. But I had to see whether they would acknowledge your death too. I wanted to know if your yearbook photo would be blown up to the size of a movie poster and placed on a black iron easel beside the others. But it wasn't. They honoured every student and teacher who died, but not you. Instead, we cremated your body two days after. I don't know if a cremation is classed as a funeral service but if it was you would have liked it - short and straight to the point. No funny anecdotes about you or depressing poems about angels and heaven. I wish I could tell you that five hundred people came, but the only people who attended were Mum and I. Not even your best friend Adam came. I'm sorry. I'm sorry for a lot of things. Maybe if I had been a better little brother then I would be watching television with you downstairs right now rather than holed up in my bedroom with the curtains closed, hunched over a journal that a therapist told me to buy.

Mrs Bell and that kid from your Chemistry class are still in the intensive care unit at the hospital. They're both expected to live, if they ever wake up. You single-handedly wiped out the rugby team. I don't think I'll miss many of them, especially not Gregory Dunn. Their glass showcase will be empty this year. No trophies, medals or team photos will fill the space. Maybe it will finally be awarded to the Music Club or the Writers' Workshop group. Maybe some of the others will finally get their chance to shine at Pembrook Academy. Is that why you did it?

I read that you walked right by the art department, without even looking in. People speculated that you didn't think anyone was in there, but I know why you did it. Anyone who really knew you would know why you skipped that wing. But that's the tragedy in this whole mess.

No one really knew you. Not even me, it seems. You always said that the art teacher Mr Allans was the only one in that whole building who acknowledged you. And I think walking on by was your final gift to him.

They released the music teacher last week after his leg surgery was successful. The gym teacher didn't make it. He died in the first week. The redhead girl that you fancied in Year Three was the last to pass away. She died on the 16th of July from 'prolonged complications'. Her parents published a full-page obituary the next week. Mum wanted to write something for you in the newspaper, but Dad wouldn't let her. He said no newspaper would print it.

I feel suffocated by the silence around me. The brutal stillness occupies every room in the house, and I can only imagine that outside is worse. Charlie, I'm dying. I can't breathe and there's no one that I can talk to. The only people who want to listen are a blurred mass of social workers, grief counsellors and journalists. And those who I reach out to are not there any more. You are not here any more. You made choices – selfish choices – that I hate you for. But then there are times that I don't hate you. There are times where I keep pounding my forehead until it bruises and aches, just to stop myself from exploding within.

My therapist says I am ' bottling up emotions which is dangerous.' Perhaps she is afraid that I will follow in your footsteps. I don't think anyone will be able to. You changed history. You made a name for yourself. You will always be remembered - well done. If this is what you wanted, you got it. You're immortalised, while the rest of us are stripped clean of any future we may have had. I hate you so much!

I don't hate you.

I don't know how I feel.

After I'm finished, I'm going to hide this. Maybe I should put my journal in your room. No one will touch it in there, especially not Dad. He's so angry at you right now, but I think that will change over time. At least, I hope so. This family will deal with hatred, remorse and bitter negativity every day of our lives. We don't need it from Dad too. He blames Mum. He blames me. He blames videogames, music and social pressures put on young people today. He even blames the school and their apparent lack of vigilance and security measures. He blames lax gun regulations that apparently make it easy for an eighteen-year-old to get access to an unlicensed handgun. The one person he does not blame is himself. He

believes he's innocent in all of this. That's why
I have to hide the journal. I don't want anyone
to read this, and know what I'm thinking. I
don't want Dad to know that I miss you. God,
I miss you so much Charlie. How am I going to
get through this?

Chapter 2

'Everything Must Go'
(Manic Street Preachers, Summer 1996)

'So, how do you feel?'

Although this was only my third session, Dr Albreck had already fed into every stereotype one could have about a therapist – leather sofa, plant in the corner of the room, box of tissues within reach, and the occasional smile and nod to remind me that she was still listening. And, of course, she always asked me, 'How do you feel?'

Honestly, I didn't know how I felt. I never did. Even if I could identify just one of the emotions that stirred within me, I wouldn't want to give it to her. All she would do with those words is write them down in her black leather notepad. She wouldn't absorb them. She wouldn't understand them. And she certainly wouldn't help me feel any differently.

'Fine,' I finally answered.

'What does "fine" mean, Sam?'

'I'm not sure how to exactly describe it. I don't have a dictionary with me.'

She smiled, although I could tell it wasn't genuine. 'What I mean is, "fine" isn't a feeling.'

I stared at her, biting my lip while waiting for a chance to unload all of my thoughts like a heavy suitcase being unpacked after a long journey. There had been so many words written in the newspapers about how my family should feel – ashamed, guilty, ignorant. It didn't matter how I felt, or what words I used to describe it because there would always be someone ready to tell me what to feel. I just wished someone would tell me what to say.

'I can see this is a difficult question for you, as usual. So, let's start with something easier. When is your first day of school?'

'Two weeks on Monday.'

'And how do you feel about that?'

There it is again – the need to talk about feelings. 'Well, I'll be starting a new school where everyone will know my name before I even step into the building, so I guess I don't feel fine.'

'Good.' She leaned forward in her chair, apparently pleased with my response. 'Sam, everyone who has faced – and survived – a traumatic event like you have finds themselves at what I like to call a "Turning Point". It's at this point where you decide whether you want to let go of everything and move forward, or stay stuck in the past. This new school could be your turning point. You should consider giving it your all. Keeping that in mind, are you planning on joining any clubs or afterschool programmes? They provide wonderful opportunities to make friends. How about the music club?'

'I was thinking of joining Teens Against Violence. What are your thoughts?' I said, crossing my arms and leaning back in the chair.

For a moment I thought she was going to smile but she didn't. 'I think that's a very good idea, Sam. Getting involved in your new school will be the fastest route to immersing yourself into that community. Immersing means – '

' – I know what immersion means.'

'Of course. You're a bright young man Sam. Are you still playing the cello?'

'Piano. Not so much, any more.' I intertwined my fingers, pressing deep into my knuckles. Resting my hands on my lap, my eyes skimmed over the walls thick with framed certificates and awards. I wondered how much each session with the great Dr Elizabeth Albreck cost. Fifty pounds an hour? Less? More? I considered asking her directly, but I had a more important question on my mind. 'How long do I have left?'

'Why do you ask?'

'Because you don't have a clock in here.' I thought that was obvious. Maybe she didn't know.

'I prefer not to remind my clients of the passing of time. I want them to feel safe and heard, without the pressure of a clock hurrying them along.'

'How do you know when the session is over?'

'It's over when it's over.'

'So, what if I was to sit here all morning?'

'Why would you do that, Sam?'

'It's just a hypothesis, Dr Albreck,' I smiled. Getting dismissed from therapy might be easier than I had thought.

'I guess I would ask you to bring whatever thoughts were going through your mind to our next session?'

'You mean, hurry me along?'

'No, not hurry you along. But *gently* inform you that I have other clients to see other than you.'

'So, you do keep track of time?'

'Not exactly. Again I don't like to remind my clients – '

' – But by "gently informing" me, you'd be reminding me of the passing of time, thus adding pressure.'

'Sam, we're getting way off topic. Let's go back to talking about your new school,' she sighed, uncrossing her legs and then re-crossing them.

'But we can't,' I shrugged, getting up off the sofa and grabbing my hoodie off the edge.

'And why is that?' she asked, sliding her glasses off her thin face that wore a tired expression.

'Because according to the large watch on your wrist that you kept glancing down at, we're all out of time.' I leaned over and popped a green mint into my mouth from the glass bowl that sat on the table by her black-skinned planner. And as I pushed open the door to the waiting room, I heard her notebook slam shut.

Unlocking my bike from the metal grid in the car park, I swung a leg over and pushed my foot down hard on the pedal. Dr Albreck's office shrank behind me until it became no more than a dot in the distance. Only seven more sessions to go. Four hundred and twenty more minutes that I would have to sit on that leather sofa and face questions that I didn't have the answers to.

The late summer wind whipped at my face, a non-existent chill stinging my skin. I pedalled harder and harder, faster and faster. The wheels spun wildly like a washing machine, going around and around. I lifted off the seat and leaned to the left, the bike curving around Knockturn Lane onto Knockothie Brae. Small square semi-detached houses lined the streets, their brick roofs blending into one thick blurry stream of red as I sped past. Around the corner into Findhorn Drive, past Market Brae, down onto Pembrook Road – I slammed the brakes on.

There it was. Pembrook Academy. How could I have gone down this way? I should've taken the right onto Golfview Road and gone past the golf course. But I didn't think. Or perhaps I did, and this was where I really wanted to be. My body was ready to confront my ghosts before I was.

My chest heaved in and out, as my lungs struggled to gasp air. Lips parted, eyes open wide, I just stared at the pale-yellow building. It was bigger than I remembered. Or maybe smaller. The rectangular windows, methodically spaced out only inches from each other, were in darkness. Wooden boards covered up the broken windows on the first floor, where students and teachers had tried to escape. A chair lay on its side, having been thrown through the window to break it. Shards of glass still lay on the tarmac beneath the frames. Yellow strips of 'Do Not Enter' tape crossed the exit doors and the main entrance. On the front steps lay a black shoe, as if someone had left it behind as they ran from the building.

Several contractors had publicly turned down the opportunity of 'refurbishing' Pembrook Academy. I guess no price was high enough to clean blood off the walls. As far as I knew, the school council was trying to hire a company from the city, where the echo of screams was slightly quieter.

I squeezed my eyes shut, biting down on my lip until I tasted warm blood. I could hear them even though I hadn't been there – the desperate screams, the frantic 999 calls, the smashing of the windows. It was so loud in my ears. I pressed my hands into my ears. 'Stop,' I whispered, 'please stop.' But it didn't stop. The screams got louder, more high-pitched, and the sound of glass shattering became deafening.

'Sam?'

I blinked my eyes open and saw the outline of someone that I used to know, someone that used to be my friend. I opened my mouth to say hello but suddenly that felt stupid. A simple hello wouldn't be enough. It wouldn't even come close.

Geoff stood in front of me, his hands trembling as they held a small bouquet of carnations wrapped in thin plastic and tied with yellow ribbon at the bottom. As my eyes skimmed the ground by his feet, I noticed more bouquets and ribbons like his. Flowers, small teddy bears and cards littered the pavement all around the perimeter of the school. Most lay on the ground, resting against the knee wall while others were tied to the metal bars of the gate. There were so many flowers, gifts, messages to loved ones and missed ones. I shouldn't have been there. I mounted my bike and turned around, slamming down on the pedals as they propelled me away from the school and the people I used to know. And from the friends I used to have.

I could hear Geoff calling to me as I pedalled faster and harder, until I reached my street. A couple of children playing skip rope in a front garden stopped when I cycled past, letting the rope drop to the ground. As I pulled into my driveway, a neighbour across the street stood frozen outside his door, groceries still in hand. I could feel his eyes burning into my back as I pushed open the front door.

'Sam, is that you?' my mum called out.

'Who else would it be,' I muttered, walking past my dad sitting in his chair with the television remote in one hand and a beer in the other. I shuffled into the kitchen and saddled into one of the bar stools.

'I had to go all the way to Watford,' she quietly said, unpacking groceries from a beige straw recycled bag, the edges frayed with use. Having been told by six retailers that she was unwelcome, Mum now needed to shop at a grocer's fifteen miles away.

I watched as she unloaded the heavy bag – milk, apples, bananas, brown sugar and cinnamon Pop

Tarts. I stared at them, the box achingly familiar.
'Mum – '

' – What is that, Linda?'

My dad carefully edged towards the kitchen
counter, setting his beer can down on the granite.
He lifted up the box of Pop Tarts, his hand slightly
trembling. 'What is this?' he asked again, hanging
on longer to each word spoken.

'Charlie will only eat the brown sugar and
cinnamon kind. He won't try any other flavour,'
she stammered, trying to grasp the box back from
Dad's hand. But he shook her off, pulling the box
in closer to his chest.

'Enough,' he whispered, squeezing his eyes shut.

'Do you remember when we tried to make him
eat the strawberry kind?' she continued, a nervous
smile stretching across her face.

'I said, enough!' He slammed the box against
the kitchen wall. It caved in upon impact, sending
small pieces of the buttery crust flying out in a dust
of sugar. It hit the floor, more large crumbs spilling
out from the broken open edges.

My mum dropped to the ground, tears spilling
from her eyes as she picked up the box and cradled
it, as if it was alive. Her back broke into tiny spasms
as her tears became louder and deeper, until they
violently shook her whole body. I waited for Dad
to walk over and comfort her, already knowing

that it wouldn't happen. He turned around and walked back to the living room, sliding into his chair and taking a long swig of beer.

I inched down from the stool and walked over to the linen cabinet. I eased out the broom and dustpan, and gingerly approached Mum on the floor. She huddled protectively over the mess. So I placed the dustpan on the floor and leaned the broom against the wall, and slumped up the stairs.

When I reached the top of the stairs, I noticed Charlie's door was slightly ajar. Not looking in, I leaned forward and closed it tight. Walking past the framed photos of him as a smiling toddler on a swing and a laughing child at Disney World, I shuffled into my bedroom and leaned on the door. I stumbled back as the door pitched and shut behind me then I slid down until my legs hit the floor and splayed out in front of me.

I tilted my head back, staring at the glow-in-the-dark stickers that had been on my ceiling for almost six years. I remembered the day Charlie and I put them up there. Dad had just taken us to the newsagent's around the corner. He did that every Wednesday after school. He said it was to help us get through the rest of the school week, although I think he also did it for himself. While he slid a six-pack of lager out from the fridge in the back of the shop, Charlie and I counted out our weekly allowance. We didn't get much, but it was always enough to pick out a comic or magazine, and a sweet.

On this particular afternoon, I had really wanted a special-edition comic about aliens and distant planets. But I didn't have enough money, even if I skipped the sweet. Charlie gave me his share. He always did stuff like that for me.

Together with our coins combined, we bought the comic and eagerly ran home with it, Dad trying to keep up behind us. While Mum cooked dinner and Dad sipped beer and watched the football highlights, Charlie and I lay on my bedroom floor and read the comic from front to back. And on the back page were free stickers that promised to glow in the dark. Charlie ripped them out, and balanced on my nightstand as I pointed out the spots in my ceiling I wanted to fill with planetary shapes and intergalactic stars.

At bedtime, when Mum thought we were brushing our teeth, we turned off the lights in the room and stared up at the ceiling in awe. They weren't bright and didn't really resemble any planets I had seen in picture books, but they were amazing. They were ours, and no matter how much we drifted apart in our later childhood years, they remained on my ceiling as a reminder of the memories we built together. Now, they reminded me of the lives that were lost that June day and of the earsplitting gunshots I heard in my head at night.

Chapter 3

'What Would the Community Think?'
(Cat Power, Autumn 1996)

The weekend flew by in a hazy stream of contorted nightmares and news headlines. My mum remained in her room for most of it. Occasionally I could hear her cries seeping in through the thin walls. My dad paced in front of the door trying to gather the strength to walk outside and face the judging looks and intentionally loud whispers of the patrons of his local pub, The Olde Black Lion. But he never left. His feet pounded the wooden floor, only briefly stopping to glance out the window, but he never walked out the door.

Before the panic could sink in, it was already there – my first day at my new school. Mum felt like it was too soon. She was worried it would come across as disrespectful to the community and those in mourning. What did they want from me? Did they want me to complete Charlie's life sentence? They couldn't have him – he was smart enough to concoct his own exit plan – so they'd take the next best thing, his brother. An eye for an eye. His blood runs in my veins too so I must be guilty along with him.

I wanted to leave this house more than anything, but my stomach churned just thinking of setting foot outside the front door. My first day at Knightsbridge Academy had thankfully been kept out of the papers, for my first week anyway. But Pembrook was a small town and in small towns people talk too much. That fact had become glaringly obvious over the past couple of months.

The cereal bowl sat full in front of me, the spoon still clean. I picked it up, scooping out the contents into the rubbish bin and placed it down into the sink, being careful not to wake my dad who snored on the living room sofa. He had slept there since it had happened, although the irreparable distance between them had grown long before the shootings.

I glanced up the stairs briefly – no one to say goodbye to. As I reached for my school bag, my hands trembled and a warm sensation filled my insides. I couldn't bring this bag today. This was the oversize rucksack that had cradled my body through my Pembrook years. This was a bag with a past, with an emotional baggage tag labelled 'heavy'. I slid it gently off the bannister and walked with it to the bin. Fabric and contents swaying gently over the lid, I opened the lid and smashed it down deep inside.

Sliding a hand into my trouser pocket, I looped some loose lining fabric around my finger like an infant searching for its comfort blanket, and stepped through the front door. A mix of rain and light mist trickled from the sky leaving a faint glistening on the grass. Snow would fall from that very sky in only a few months. That was Charlie's favourite time of the year. He loved painting the streets blanketed in soft white. I wondered if his paintings were still in the art room. I bet they were dry by now, but there would be no one to bring them home.

Pushing away memories of the winters past, I hurried down the street to the bus stop on the corner of Windham Drive. I had been told in the orientation letter that bus 09 would go right to the new school. Seventeen miles and 40 minutes later, the bus flew past the tall black gates of Knightsbridge Academy.

'Excuse me?' I leaned forward and loudly cleared my throat. 'This is my stop,' I called out. No response. I stood up and shuffled to the front, my legs wobbling underneath me as I shifted from side to side. 'That was my stop,' I said again, pointing to the school in the rear-view mirror.

As the brakes suddenly slammed on, my body hurtled forwards, hitting a silver pole. The driver turned around to face me. 'Sorry, didn't see you sitting way back there...'

When I looked up, I saw him staring at me with wide eyes and a gaping mouth, like I was an animal at the zoo. Interesting, amusing, but unpredictable and therefore dangerous. Does everyone know my face? Do I look like my brother?

Scrambling to my feet, I hurried down the stairs hearing the squeak of my soles on the wet rubber lining. When my shoes touched the slippery concrete, I felt the urge to look back. I couldn't help it. I needed to know. So I did.

'My neighbour's grandson went to Pembrook Academy,' he said, his eyes suddenly dark. Then he spat on the steps of the bus, shut the doors and drove away, leaving me standing there in my shame and confusion.

By the time I got to Knightsbridge Academy, it was 8.40am. I would need to leave earlier the next day. Maybe if I walked a little further from the house I could take a different bus. I would wear my hood up over my face so the new driver wouldn't recognise me. Who knows how he would be connected – maybe his daughter's friend went to Pembrook Academy, or his postman's nephew taught there. Everyone seemed to be just one more piece of this intricate puzzle, waiting for their turn to be noticed and slotted into the big picture.

When I got to school, the main doors were already locked. I had to use a buzzer to get inside and when I did I had to go through a metal detector like at the airport. Knightsbridge Academy had clearly stepped up its security since June. Or, perhaps it was only installed after they heard of my enrollment here.

A stout secretary with curls on her head and above her upper lip greeted me in the office with a forced smile. 'Samuel Macmillan?'

'Yeah,' I said, gripping the strap on my bag until the fabric pinched my palm.

'You're late.'

I nodded, noticing how her voice quivered slightly when she addressed me. Was she scared of me?

Quickly averting her eyes, she handed me a white envelope. 'School begins promptly at 8.05am but since this is your first day, we'll give you a pass. Here is your timetable. English has already started so show your late pass to the teacher. Room 212.'

Beyond the office, the building opened up into a large hall with high ceilings. Peach tiled flooring stretched out and disappeared under several closed doors that were interspersed around the hall. The ceiling was comprised of long glass panels angled into a peak, like the steeple of a church. The walls were dotted with framed awards, certificates and the occasional art project. It didn't look much different to Pembrook Academy.

Seeing a student come out of one of the classroom doors, I hurried towards him. 'Excuse me, where's the stairs?'

He opened his mouth to respond then his eyes darted to the white envelope in my hand, and my name written in bold font across it.

'Find it yourself,' he said, gently pushing past me.

After several loops around the hall, I finally found the stairwell. Peering into classrooms, the envelope already damp from my sweaty hands, I tiptoed down the hall on the second floor. Each step mimicked the wild pounding of my heartbeat and every room I passed seemed to shift towards me, as if the walls were slowly closing in. By the time I had reached room 212, I had sweated through my T-shirt and my flannel shirt. My breathing was heavy and loud, and alarmingly erratic. I hadn't realised that I would be this nervous. If I had, I probably wouldn't have left the house.

Palm slick on the shiny silver doorknob, I opened the door and cautiously stepped over the threshold. Fourteen heads instantly spun around to look at me. I opened my mouth to weakly announce myself, but the teacher stopped me.

'We've been expecting you. Take a seat.'

Locating the last seat in the back row, I plopped down on the wooden chair. My body suddenly drained of energy, the anxiety depleting my reserves, I rested my back against the wood.

The teacher loudly cleared his throat, gaining back the attention of at least half of the class. The rest eventually turned back around after they got bored of waiting for me to do something.

'As I was saying, due to the recent... incident... we will be working from a new text list for our American Literature unit. Please dispose of your old ones – '

' – Excuse me, Sir? What if we've already read the books from the old list?' called out a mousy brunette from the second row.

'Loser.' A few kids from the back rows laughed, and looked at the student they knew had said it.

'That's enough, Noel. For those who have already read the texts from the old list, please talk to the headteacher for credit.'

'What books are off the list?' asked another student seated near the window. Looking around I saw that all the window blinds were down, shielding those inside. Not even a sliver of daylight snaked in from under the horizontal slats. But judging from people's expressions, the threat wasn't lurking outside. It was inside, sitting in the back row. I shifted in my chair and pulled at my shirt collar, feeling the heat from their silent stares.

'*One Flew Over the Cuckoo's Nest*; *The Catcher in the Rye*.' He cleared his throat suddenly, 'And we won't be studying Truman Capote's *In Cold Blood*,' he said, not meaning to send a glance my way. But he did. And everyone saw.

'But those are classics!' shouted one boy from the middle row, which set off a wave of comments and frustrated outbursts.

'What are we going to be reading instead? Children's books?'

'This is meant to be Advanced English, not nursery school.'

'Why are we getting punished for something that *he* did?' said Noel loudly.

'He'? Is he talking about me, or Charlie?

The class fell silent, and slowly heads turned over frigid shoulders, looking back at me. My toes squirmed in my shoes and I tucked my chin to my chest, avoiding their piercing eyes, their angry thoughts, their fears. Glancing down at the floor beneath my desk, I wished I were back home in my bedroom, hidden under my covers where no one could find me.

'If anyone has anything to say, you can talk to

Ms Bevins. I don't make the rules. In the meantime, let's get back to the current syllabus: Shakespeare.'

After that, English class flew by in a haze of discomfort, as did Physics then Maths. This Noel kid ended up being in most of my classes, and had a comment to say in almost every one. And just when I thought I had peaked, the day got progressively worse. At lunch, a pretty raven-haired girl from the year above walked over to me. I was sitting at a long thin metal folding table, six empty seats to my left and to my right, and this girl chose to sit right beside me. At first, I was confused then surprised, and by the end I was even optimistic. She turned to me, smiled sweetly with her cherry-stained lip-gloss and asked, 'Are you Sam Macmillan?'

Of course, I was beginning to get excited at this point and probably too quickly nodded my head. Then she said, 'This is for Pembrook,' before pouring most of her ice-cold Diet Coke into my lap. She threw the remainder of it, with the paper cup and straw, into my lunch tray, making my food completely inedible. She laughed, then walked away to join Noel and his friends sitting at the table beside me, who high-fived her.

I battled with whether to stand up, let the ice cubes fall from my lap and walk away, or remain seated until after the lunch bell rang. I stayed in my chair – bad choice. By the time the bell rang and everyone rushed by me, my lap was filled with half-eaten sandwiches, more ice-cold drinks and even the odd apple core. I was a human rubbish bin, and that too was how I was beginning to see myself. And despite what Dr Albreck said, it didn't get much better.

Having only 're-immersed' myself back into the archaic ritualistic behaviours of a teenager for a couple of weeks, I was already aware of my status at this school and the divide that it caused. The student population here seemed to be partitioned into three distinct groupings. For purposes of convenience, I called them Group A, Group B and Group N/A, where the current ranking was as the label states, 'Non-Applicable'. Unfortunately, Group A had attracted the bigger number – those who hated the sight of me. They had no qualms about conveying this to me, at most times of the day and in most places in the building. The raven-haired drink-wielding girl was certainly a member of this group, seemingly led by Noel. Those who tripped me in the halls passed hate notes to me in class and frequently knocked into me while I walked, were also members of this group.

Group B consisted of primarily girls and highly sensitive theatre-driven boys whose heightened emotional awareness prevented them from looking me in the eye or acknowledging my presence in classes. Often they walked by me with a glistening in their eye and a slight trembling of the bottom lip. That group didn't bother me, and I was happy to avoid them if that's what they wanted. It was the third group that fascinated me the most – the non-applicable group. Those were the ones who rimmed their eyes in dark liner, wore various music shirts depicting album logos and who spent their afternoons after school sitting on the steps at the High Street Art Gallery debating which Radiohead song best defines the decline of modern society. They were the ones who occasionally and nonchalantly passed glances my way and who didn't seem to display any of the typical responses that I had grown accustomed to: anger, hatred, fear, confusion. It was Group N/A that I decided to sit next to at Free Period one day.

At first, no one looked my way as I slid into an empty seat, but when my geometry book slid out of my hands and onto the floor loudly, that's when they took notice. It was easy to see who the group leader was because many glanced towards one particular boy who sat at the head of the table, his eyes fixed on me. Some flitted between him and me, while others waited for his response to influence theirs. But instead of telling me to leave, he grinned at me and continued his conversation.

'So, my cousin says he can get us in around 10 tonight.'

'I don't know, Dougie. I'm still grounded from last weekend,' shrugged one of the other boys who I would later find out was nicknamed Worm.

'So, tell your dad that you're going to the library to finish a Physics project,' chimed in a pretty brunette sitting beside Dougie with her arm around the back of his chair. Her eyes were wide and her lashes were so long they skimmed her eyebrows when she glanced up at me occasionally. I didn't know why but she made my cheeks burn slightly.

'He'll never buy that,' Worm scoffed.

'Then tell him you'd be happy to finish it at home but that Sam here is your Physics partner,' she grinned, winking at me.

'Sam Macmillan!' he blurted out, as if my name caused him physical pain. 'My dad would never let him in the house.' He quickly glanced at me. 'No offence, I don't even know you.'

'Exactly. The library will sound pretty nice to your dad then,' she laughed.

'So, it's settled,' the group's leader announced loudly, silencing the others beside him. 'We'll meet at Griffins Park at 9.30 and get the bus over.' He shoved a couple of books into his torn leather backpack and stood up from the table, pushing away the chair. Immediately, everyone else followed. But before they left, he turned to me and in front of everyone, talked directly to me. 'You coming with us?'

I looked around to see if there was someone else he could be talking to. 'Me?'

'Yeah, you. My cousin is a bartender at this music club in the city and there's a good band playing on Saturday.'

'I don't have a fake ID,' I answered quickly, hoping that would be the end of the conversation.

'Neither do we.'

Every immediate excuse in my mind induced some elaborate story that would mean talking out loud for a long time to a group of people staring at me. So, to avoid more embarrassment, I just nodded.

'Good. See you at Griffins Park. We meet at the big slide.'

Their backs turned, I replayed that conversation over and over in my head. But no matter how much I analysed each word exchanged, I couldn't make sense of what just happened. I opened my mouth to call them back, explain that I couldn't make it Saturday night. But then I realised – I wanted this. I wanted to go with them. But did they really want me there? Was this my big turning point? Or was I about to find out that

I hadn't actually reached the bottom, and that I could, in fact, fall much deeper into the hole that my brother had dug for me?

Chapter 4

'The Circle' *(Ocean Colour Scene, Autumn 1996)*

Saturday couldn't come fast enough. Noel and his group of followers continued their efforts to make my days at Knightsbridge increasingly difficult. In P.E., a 'friendly' basketball game turned into an unfriendly game of dodgeball where I was the target. Noel and his friends bumped me in Chemistry, causing a beaker to drop to the ground and green liquid to ooze out. Somehow it was me that gained a one-day detention for that. Again, I was a human rubbish bin at lunchtime, and just when I thought the week couldn't get any worse, someone wrote 'R.I.P. Pembrook' on my notebook in English when I went to the bathroom.

When Saturday finally arrived, I was so anxious I didn't eat all day. Several scenarios surrounding Saturday's plans raced through my mind, ones where I would say something witty and everyone would love me, and others where I would show up at Griffins Park and no one would be there. Regardless of tonight's outcome, one thing was clear. For the first time in a long time, I was thinking about something else other than my brother and what he did. And no one would ever understand how amazing that felt.

Outfit after outfit hit my bedroom floor but not one looked or felt right. It was too warm for the striped jumper that had patches on the elbows from too much wear, and the collared shirt made me look like I was going to church. All of my shoes looked too polished, and my hair resisted the gel I squeezed into it. I took so long picking out an outfit that I missed dinner, but apparently no one downstairs noticed. I wasn't even that hungry, and it gave me more time to choose between blue jeans or beige cords. I chose the cords, which I instantly regretted as soon as I walked up to the slide. They turned up – which squashed one theory – but they were all wearing the same outfit near enough – black jeans, a graphic tee and a ripped flannel shirt turned up at the sleeves. Each had on an array of leatherette wrist accessories, loose strands effortlessly looping around another band or simply just sticking out.

'You came,' smiled the girl, as she turned around. Should I not have?

She jumped off the slide and took a step closer. 'I'm Izzy, and this is Dougie.'

Dougie, the leader, leaned up against the steps of the big slide and simply acknowledged my presence by nodding. The others followed suit, each offering up their own identity – Worm, Max, Debbie, Neall. And there I was, just Sam. No cool nicknames or funny anecdotes to follow. Before I had time to question myself any more, we were off. Hopping onto the 39 bus, we occupied the back row of seats as regular teens do on a Saturday night.

It was a little after ten o'clock when we reached the music hall. I didn't want to mention that I usually went to bed by nine. The queue of people spread over a whole block, showcasing an eclectic mix of facial piercings and neck tattoos. Instead of joining the back of the line, Dougie led us around the back of the building past the rubbish bins. We huddled outside the back door and waited almost twenty minutes in awkward silence before the door opened, hitting Worm in the face. Standing in the doorway was a lanky guy in his mid-twenties with a chain that seemed to be painfully and unnecessarily connected from his right nostril to his right ear lobe.

'You brought too many. I said three, max.'

'Come on, there's only six of us,' pleaded Dougie.

'Seven,' corrected Izzy, motioning towards me.

I could feel people's eyes on me, so I lowered my head until part of my face was hidden in the collar of my coat.

'Fine but if anyone catches you, you tell them you sneaked in. OK?'

Dougie shrugged and slid past his cousin. 'Didn't even see you.'

Inside, music blasted from all around me, crushing my head like heavy stone. It would take at least a couple of days for my ears to stop ringing. Sweaty bodies danced too close to each other and flipped their heads back and forth to a song that seemed to consist only of screaming and loud banging.

'Do you like punk rock?' screamed Izzy over the noise.

'Love it!' I yelled back at her, possibly too quickly. Was punk rock a sub-genre of rock? Or, did it refer to a specific band? Honestly, I hated whatever was happening on the stage in front of me. Aside from the singer who was dressed in a torn tuxedo, there was no real music to be found. Ten years of piano lessons had embarrassingly left me with only a preference for the classics. And whatever this was, it was definitely not classical.

Within fifteen minutes, I had found my place for the next three hours – in a corner by the men's bathroom. While Debbie flailed her arms around on the dancefloor like she was having an epileptic fit, Worm, Max and Neall bartered to get two older guys to buy them beers. I hadn't seen Dougie since we walked in. Eyes scanning the room, I searched for him and Izzy. When a group of dancers left the floor for another round of some white-coloured liquid that was served in a test tube that belonged in a chemistry lab, I saw her. Standing alone by the stairs, Izzy stared out momentarily transfixed. Her face glistened in the strobe lights, and she clenched her jaw. Glancing over my shoulder, I saw Dougie propped against the bar, beer in hand, talking to two girls. One had red streaks in her hair and the other had a lip ring. Whatever he was saying must have been funny, because they were laughing and throwing their heads back.

When I looked back at the stairs, Izzy was gone. I wouldn't see her again until the end, when we all met up back at the exit.

'Dougie, where were you all night?' asked Worm.

'Who's hungry?' grinned Dougie, as he headed out the exit.

Three streets down and one street left, I found myself inside a 24-hour cafe near the city bus station. Izzy had clearly forgiven Dougie because they were holding hands by the time we got a booth for seven people.

I sat down in the chair at the end of the booth,

while the others poured onto the frayed red leather benches. Menus lay on the table in front of us and I could see that the top one had a sticky red stain, like tomato sauce. My fingers pressed into the edges of the chair until I awkwardly looped them together on my lap. Looking at Dougie's faded black David Bowie T-shirt and torn plaid shirt, I was suddenly very aware of my appearance. The round collar on my saggy navy-blue jumper itched and I squirmed uncomfortably in my beige cords.

Izzy sat directly to my right, huddled into Dougie as his arm carelessly hung around her shoulders. In the fluorescent overhead lights, I could see that her eyes were thickly rimmed with black liner. It made her eyes look smaller than they were. Debbie had told me that Izzy only started hanging out with them last year, that before that she was 'Isabel' and too popular to even acknowledge them. I had asked Debbie why that was, but all she said was Izzy had 'had a bad year'. Then one morning she came to school and she was different. It was as if she'd woken up and decided to become a new person. Soon she started going out with Dougie, dyed her hair black, began organising student rights protests about better food sourcing for the cafeteria and became fixated on the 1970s era. Now she looked like Deborah Harry, with her thick make-up and dyed hair cut short with a heavy long fringe resting on her eyelids. I don't know why she picked the 1970s. Perhaps she didn't know that it was a period heavily shadowed by the Vietnam War and social propaganda.

'You hungry, Sam? See anything you like?' she asked, a wide grin stretching across her face. Did she see me looking at her?

I quickly looked away, before Dougie saw me staring too. 'I don't know,' I mumbled. Honestly, I didn't know if I was hungry. I was only hungry if everyone else was and I would only order a drink if someone else did. But the waitress approached me first.

After a few moments of silence and an exchange of glances around the table, the waitress finally snapped. 'Are you going to order something or not?' she said.

I looked to Dougie for some sort of cue to what I should order, but he was staring across the table at Debbie and Neall with a smirk and a slight gleam in his irises.

'Well?' the waitress hissed, her pink lipstick smearing across her front teeth.

'Um... I... just a bowl of cornflakes with milk,' I eventually stammered. I hadn't looked at the menu and didn't even know if cereal was available, but at the time it seemed like an appropriate choice. It wasn't. The whole table erupted in laughter and my face burned red. When I looked away from my sweaty palms in my lap, I saw that the only one who wasn't still laughing was Dougie.

'Make that two bowls of cornflakes,' he added, still smirking.

The laughter faded out as the waitress scribbled down six more orders of cornflakes before tearing off the sheet and begrudgingly handing it through the open hatch to the kitchen. She looked back over at our table, and rolled her eyes contentiously the way my brother used to whenever Dad tried to talk to him after a few beers. After a while, the only person Charlie talked to was me. And soon that stopped too.

After a few minutes of steady silence, the waitress came back over and slammed down seven individually wrapped boxes of cornflakes, seven bowls, spoons and a jug of milk. Quietly everyone began pouring their cereal, sneaking small smiles back and forth. Finally, Dougie slammed his spoon down on the table, and with cornflakes falling out of his mouth, he yelled, 'You're so weird, Sam. I love it!'

Soon several chaotic conversations ensued, my eyes darting back and forth hungrily consuming all of them. Dougie and Max were talking about a music band I'd never heard of, and Debbie was showing Izzy her newly tattooed wrist, which was covered in tiny blue stars. On top of that, Debbie would intermittently interrupt Max to chime in with her opinions of the depiction of women in music videos, while Izzy and Dougie shared the occasional inside joke and stolen exchange. Worm and Max competed for the best impersonation of John Major, while Neall talked even louder to block out Debbie's voice.

I'd never been to a tennis match but I would imagine that it would be close to what I was experiencing. After a few minutes, my neck ached so I started counting through my pennies to pay the bill. I immediately wished I had brought more so I could have paid for the whole bill, rather than just for my measly share. Maybe they would want to hang out with me again if I paid the whole bill. I would remember that next time. A dull ache suddenly grew in my belly – would there be a next time?

I was still kicking myself for not bringing more money when I noticed that Izzy was lagging behind the group on the walk home. She seemed to have slowed her steps to walk with me, but I knew there had to be another reason. She occasionally glanced up and smiled, before eventually nudging me. 'I'm really glad you came tonight.'

When I looked up, I noticed tiny dimples in the

corners of her smile. Her eyes were bright even in the darkness. 'How are you enjoying Knightsbridge?'

'It's OK,' I mumbled. Maybe she did want to walk with me. My palms started to sweat and I resisted rubbing them on my trousers in front of her.

'I went to nursery with Noel Taylor and he hasn't changed one bit,' she laughed. 'He's an idiot, and he enjoys making people's lives miserable so don't worry about him. He'll get bored soon.'

'Yeah, she should know. She went out with him!' yelled Debbie from in front of us. 'Sam, why are you sixteen and in our year? Did you get moved up or something?'

'Yeah, Pembrook moved me up,' I said, feeling a stare from Dougie.

'You must be really smart. Cool. Why did you move from…?' she continued, quickly trailing off before she got elbowed in the ribs by Max. 'Sorry, Sam. I forgot –'

'– It's fine, really,' I shrugged, not knowing what else to say.

'Have you checked out the old art theatre yet? It got refurbished last year, only just opened,' Izzy said, eyeing up Debbie who was still blushing from embarrassment.

I slowly shook my head. 'What do they show there?'

'Old films, foreign films. In the lobby they sell retro sweets. Do you like Roman Polanski?'

'Yes,' I said. Of course I was lying. Was that a retro sweet or had I missed the transition into another topic?

'Maybe we can all go see a film sometime?' she asked, a genuine smile beaming across her face.

I hadn't watched a movie since Pembrook, but I didn't know whether that was because I was so preoccupied with my own thoughts, or whether movies just seemed frivolous to me now. There was more violence, drama and tragedy in my life. I didn't really need to watch a movie. I could just turn on the news and see the latest Charlie report.

Before I could tell her that I'd love to go to the cinema with her, Worm jumped in a puddle and sent sprays of muddy water towards Debbie. Screaming something about a vintage skirt, she stormed off. When we got to the bus stop, she was sitting on the bench wiping mud streaks off her skirt. Leaning against the doorway of the bus shelter, I glanced at Izzy and noticed that she was staring back at me and smiling.

I hadn't really responded to her question. And even though it unnerved me not knowing who I was or what I liked any more, I still went to bed early that morning with her words burning sweetly into my thoughts. And when I awoke early in the afternoon, I discovered both a broken framed photo of Charlie at the bottom of the stairs, and that my parents hadn't even noticed that I had gone out the night before.

Chapter 5

'6 Underground' *(Sneaker Pimps, Autumn 1996)*

Peering over the top of my notepad, I saw Dr Albreck's almond-shaped hazel eyes flitting from my shaking foot to the pen twirling in my fingers. Two swirling masses of greenish-browns burrowing into my thoughts, watching my every move, analysing each moment. Catching her eyes, my attention darted back down to the notebook.

A low humming seeped out of the monitor on her table, and from somewhere in the waiting room, I heard a phone ringing. A slight breeze flowed through the trees, making some of the branches bend and sway. Peeling my eyes away from the window, I checked back to see if Dr Albreck was still watching me. She was.

'Ready?'

She'd decided on a new approach for today's session since I had spent the previous appointment attempting to inquire about her personal life.

Although perhaps invasive and rude at times, I thought the questions were reasonable, and warranted. How was I supposed to confess my deepest darkest thoughts to a woman who I knew nothing about? Perhaps she too harboured some dark notions that made her emotionally incapable of helping me with mine.

Unfortunately, she was less than forthcoming about her marital status, university grades and personal food preferences, which left me still unsure of her capabilities to assist me during the worst time of my life. That day she had ended the appointment early – without offering me a reimbursement of the minutes retracted – and changed the direction of the next session.

This afternoon I was to write down three emotions I had felt in the past week. Since I had arrived twelve minutes late for our therapy session because of the late night I had had the evening before, the first emotion on my list was remorse. After that, the page was blank.

'Sam?'

'I'm having a difficult time collecting my thoughts.'

'Do you have anything written down?'

'Yes, remorse.'

'Excellent. Let's start with that. Tell me why you think you felt remorse this week?'

'Because I was twelve minutes late today and I really dislike people who aren't punctual.'

She took a long deep breath, and then straightened back up. 'Do you feel remorse for anything else? The events of the past year, perhaps?'

I felt my body retreat, my spine pushing into the back of the armchair until it became uncomfortable. A bitter taste in my mouth caused me to swallow, but I couldn't get rid of it. Was she implying that I should feel remorse for my brother's actions? I thought I was coming here to let go of feelings of guilt and blame, not to accept them. One emotion suddenly became clear to me – anger. But instead of writing it down or simply saying what I was thinking, I did exactly what I had been doing for the past few sessions. Afraid of the discussions being about me, my family, I turned it back on her. 'Have you ever felt remorse? Maybe for something that you did in your past?'

'Sam, like I told you last time, these sessions aren't about me. They're about you.'

'Right, I remember,' I said, my response sounding sharper than I'd intended.

She uncrossed her legs and re-crossed them in another way, her eyebrows pinching together. Taking another deep breath, she dropped her pen on her notepad as if surrendering. 'Sam, do you think you'd be more comfortable talking with another counsellor? Maybe a male counsellor?'

'Are you... firing me? Am I being fired from therapy? Can that even happen?'

'Not fired, but transferred to a more suitable pairing. And it can happen if the client would feel more comfortable meeting with another psychologist. Of course, I want to keep seeing you but I worry that our sessions aren't moving forward. I want you to feel that this is a safe space where you can talk about anything. I want these sessions to help you, and I don't think they are.'

'Sure, if that's what you want?'

'Again, it's not about me, it's about you.'

What did she want me to say? No? Did she want me to beg? So, I responded in the only way I knew how, 'Um... OK?'

She paused, as if she wanted to say something more but instead picked up her pen to make her final notes. Head down, she continued talking to me without meeting my eyes. 'OK. So I will make a recommendation to one of my colleagues who I feel would be a good communication partner for you and he will contact you to arrange therapy days and times.' She finally looked up at me, her eggshell-coloured frames sliding down the bridge of her nose slightly. 'Sam, do you have anything you'd like to say or ask me before we end our last session? And no, I don't mean ask me a question about my personal life.'

Chewing on the inside of my cheek, I considered the many questions that pushed against my head causing me pain, but couldn't find the right one to ask. So, I said nothing and shook my head in silence.

'Right. Well, good luck, Sam. I hope you find more success in your next therapy,' she said, standing up. She smoothed down the front of her skirt and readjusted her glasses. Even though she tried to hide it with her thick glasses, too-tight bun that pinched at her scalp and beige clothing, she was pretty. And there was something about her that made me feel comfortable in her office. Had she not given up so easily, I may have actually opened up to her someday. But like all the adults in my life, she was too busy to wait. Asking her too many personal questions – strike one. Arriving late to a session – strike two. Failing to immediately spill my thoughts, fears and the crushing weight of grief to her – strike three. Three strikes and I was out.

Leaving the notepad on my seat, blank except for one word written on it: Remorse, I slumped out of her office feeling like I'd just failed an exam. I considered turning back to wave, but a strange feeling of the very emotion that I had written down washed over me and I didn't want her to see. I didn't want to go. I wanted to tell her to just be patient for a little while longer. I wanted to explain to her that this was how everyone in my family handled their emotions, by bottling them up until they explode like a shaken Coke bottle. But like my family, I was too stubborn to apologise, too scared to ask for help, and too selfish to care. So, I walked straight to the exit door and pushed it open, not turning back to see if it closed properly behind me.

The next morning, I awoke to the usual muffled voices of my parents from the kitchen. Although the conversation was brief and void of emotion, they didn't seem to be fighting today. Perhaps we'd have a normal Sunday morning, like a normal family who dealt with normal problems, like whose turn it was to do the dishes or whether there were enough whites to do a light-coloured load of laundry.

'Sam?'

'Yeah, Dad?'

'I'm going to need you to go to the library today. Just between 10am and 2pm.'

'Why?'

'We're having an open house for prospective buyers today.'

'You never told me that,' my mum said, turning around to face him. My dad ignored her and continued making his coffee. 'Dan? You never told me.' Her voice was getting louder, more desperate.

'What does it matter?'

'I just didn't think we were in a rush to sell?'

'Of course we are. We can't stay here. Do you know I got my headlights smashed out again?'

'Why don't you park in the garage then?' I shrugged, sliding a cup towards my dad for him to fill with strong black coffee. He ignored me.

'I'm not ready to sell, Dan,' my mum blurted out suddenly.

So much for my normal Sunday morning. I braced myself for my dad's response, moving my empty coffee mug out of the line of fire.

'I'm not getting into this right now.'

'You're not listening. I'm not ready,' she said again.

'The sign's been up for weeks! And now you tell me?'

'I didn't think we'd have any interest this soon. I thought because of the journalists still outside that it would take months, maybe even a year? I thought we had more time here.'

'Well, we do have interest. Two people have already contacted the agent.'

'So cancel!'

'We're having the open house today. I'm not cancelling. And that's the end of it.'

'And what about me?' she cried.

'For once, let's not make this about you,' he snapped, slamming down his coffee cup. Drops of black liquid seeped over the edge and trickled down the cup, forming a circle on the tile. After he went into the garage and Mum stormed upstairs, slamming the door behind her, I cleaned up the coffee with a dampened rag by the sink, worried that it would stain.

Quickly showering and throwing on some jeans, I packed a bag with textbooks and a notepad and jogged to the bus stop. But instead of taking bus 09 to Knightsbridge town centre for the library, I took bus 11 to Priory Road in Pembrook, where the town's cemetery was located.

When I got off the bus, a dark gloomy cloud hung in the sky and seemed to follow me overhead. I hadn't worn my raincoat, but whether it rained or not was the furthest thought from my mind. A path snaked around the cemetery and eventually led to the back section where a dozen new graves sat. Slowly making my way from one to the other, I read each headstone carefully, absorbing the names, the birthdates, the messages from their loved ones. Too many deaths. Too much loss. Mr Healey, Gregory, Mr Smith, Nick, David M., David R., Stephen, Laura, Michael, Cara, Geoff, Andrew, Robert, Joseph. There they all were, six feet underground, beneath the soles of my shoes as if they'd never existed at all. It was like their voices had never carried in the hallways, as if their laughter hadn't filled the classrooms. But they had existed. I had seen them. I had heard them. And now they were reduced to merely bones and decaying flesh.

I hadn't thought much about the afterlife before that morning in June. The theory of heaven and hell isn't exactly a popular discussion topic for teenagers. When you're sixteen years old, death isn't a possibility. It's a story that you read about in the news, a sadness that spreads through hospitals, a tragedy that frequently visits the elderly, but never the young. Death should never meet the young. But it did. Thanks to my brother, death made fourteen new friends that day. Maybe even fifteen, if you count Charlie. But I don't think death came for him. I think something darker and more sinister took his soul. When I imagine those students looking down, like that dark cloud above, I know my brother isn't with them. I don't know where he is.

Walking over to section B of the cemetery, I glanced back at the new graves as they withered into rows of stone and fresh flowers. Section B was starkly different, its headstones made of remnant material and the flower bouquets reduced to a single stem. And there it was. It looked smaller, less worthy of the attention it had gathered. No amount of protest and headline could stop the development of Charlie's stone. I didn't know why people had got so angry. His body wasn't even buried there. We had had him cremated, as he wished, with the intention of scattering his ashes at Harper's Beach, where we had played as children. But the urn still sat on my mother's bedside table, allowing her a place to think of my brother, away from my dad's judging eyes and my face, which reminded her too much – and not enough – of Charlie's. But my parents, or rather my mum, had decided on a granite bevel marker to represent a place of rest. As per my dad's wishes, she had kept it simple: his name, date of birth and date of death. No message or prayer, just facts.

When I got to my brother's stone, I dropped to my knees. Someone had poured soil on top and garnished it with headless thorny rose stems. Scooping the earth off, I polished the granite beneath with the sleeve of my jumper until a pale greyish blue shone through. Words sizzled in my mouth, rising to the surface, but when I opened my mouth, images of fourteen graves entered my mind. So I left the cemetery, having not done what I had gone there to do – forgive my brother.

I returned home earlier than I should have. Not even one o'clock. A silver Jeep Cherokee sat in the driveway. I quietly sneaked in and up the stairs, hearing my dad talk business to a guy who looked to be in his twenties. He looked a little young to be buying a house, especially for this neighbourhood. But when I reached the top, it quickly sunk in why he was there. Positioned in the doorway, almost too afraid to step any closer, was a young woman taking photos of my brother's room.

'You should leave before my dad catches you,' I said, as she spun around, dropping the camera by her feet.

'I… I was just…' But she didn't finish her sentence, unable to find a good reason to explain why she was doing what she was doing. She grabbed her camera, called down to her boyfriend and hurried to the Jeep. I met my dad at the front door just in time to see their car reach the end of the street, tyre streaks still visible on the concrete.

'Dad, they were – '

' – I know.' He sighed and rubbed his forehead. 'I know, Sam.' He sauntered back into the kitchen, grabbed a beer from the fridge and quietly closed the garage door behind him. A minute later, I heard him slam something hard against the door. He would later emerge that afternoon in need of a bandage to cover his bloody fist.

Chapter 6

'Head Over Feet' *(Alanis Morissette, Autumn, 1996)*

'I'm going out!' I yelled up the stairs. I was trying a new approach. Rather than sulk in a corner, I would dance in front of them like a circus animal until they noticed me.

'I won't be back until late. Probably around midnight or 1am.' No response. 'It might be dangerous out there. There could be lurkers... lurking.' OK, so this wasn't going to plan. Had Mum even heard me? Did they remember I still lived here?

I pulled open the garage door and saw my dad hovering over a voltage box with a pair of pliers and a screwdriver in his hands. A pint glass of lager sat on the wooden workbench behind him, one third full.

'Dad? I'm heading out.'

'Right.'

'I won't be back until late so don't wait up.'

'Right.'

I waited around for him to ask me where I was going and why I wasn't going to be back until late. And whether I had enough money in case I needed to take a taxi home, and if I was going to be warm enough in only a T-shirt in November. After a few minutes, he glanced up at me standing in the doorway awkwardly. 'What?' he asked.

Right. That's it, I guess. Nothing more to say.

Debbie's house was about a ten-minute walk from the school bus stop, Dougie had told me. Hunched over his note, passed to me in Physics on Thursday during theoretical discussions of kinetic motion, I reread it for the twentieth time. His Fs looped and curled inwards and his Ss lazily hung down. But even after the twentieth time, I questioned whether the note was for me. Perhaps it was for the boy that sat behind me, or the girl who sat at the table next to me. Why would it be for me? Why would I be invited to a 'hang out' on Friday night? I was nobody.

I had gone to sleep that Thursday night with the note tucked under my pillow, as if the wish wouldn't come true without it. I thought I'd blown it by the time the note came to me. I had seen them earlier that week in the hallways and at the cafeteria but they'd been deep in conversation and

I hadn't wanted to interrupt them. By Thursday morning, I was sick with anxiety. I wanted so badly to be friends with them. The only thing that had the potential of pulling me out of this nightmarish hole was Dougie and Izzy. Without them my future at Knightsbridge Academy was bleak, like the many headlines splashed across the local newspapers that week.

A part of me wondered how I must appear. I could see myself from the outside, looking desperate and socially hungry. But I couldn't stop. I needed them to like me. I needed them to want me. I just needed to be needed, for once.

I had even got the bus to the city center the day after the music club and bought a faded grey Ramones T-shirt from the too-cool-for-me records store on Abbot Avenue. The shop assistant had given me the 'raised eyebrow' for a long and visible moment before ringing up the sale. I had tried not to cough at the forty-quid price tag that came with being quirky and innovative.

So there I was, freezing to death in my Ramones T-shirt and a pair of my favourite jeans that I had cut up with my mum's kitchen scissors, counting the houses on Herron Crescent. There it was, number 42. Light flickered from inside the house, sporadically illuminating the windows through the thin lace curtains. The TV must have been on. For a split second it hit me that this was a moment that I'd never be able to tell my big brother about. This was one memory that I'd never get to share with him, nor ask his advice for next time. I was on my own. That fact was becoming clearer every day.

Palms already slick with sweat, I took a deep breath and pressed the doorbell. Voices got louder and footsteps got nearer, and after what seemed like an hour to me the door flew open.

Standing in the doorframe wearing a pair of baggy torn jeans that hung around her hip bones and a tight black vest, was Izzy. Tall glass tumbler in one hand and half a cigarette in the other, she smiled at me and I felt the whole universe crumble below my feet.

'Hey,' I said, a little too loudly and casually. I didn't know what to do with my hands so I awkwardly placed them on my hips. Stupid idea.

She laughed and gestured me inside. 'Come in through, Sam. Nice shirt, by the way.'

Shuffling through the dimly lit hallway, I heard a mix of loud music and even louder conversations from beyond the door at the end. Terracotta wallpaper and mismatched frames with photos of a buck-toothed Debbie from all ages were scattered on the walls. The carpet beneath my soles was slightly sticky with something I didn't want to know about.

Pushing the door open, I saw the group laughing and throwing back brown and yellow liquids from expensive-looking glasses. In the middle of the group was Dougie. Dressed in tight-fitting jeans, a charcoal-coloured MTV tee and finished with a crisp white blazer jacket, he radiated self-assurance in a way I never thought possible. He was incredible.

He stretched his arms out wide when he saw me, and the group instantly quieted. 'Sam! Welcome to a Friday Frenzy!' I was to learn much later in the evening that they all did this every Friday night, albeit rain or snow. They discussed the location of the next Friday Frenzy on Monday mornings, each checking in with their parents to see who would be working late or out at the pub drinking their salary away. Ever since Debbie's parents divorced, her mum had been frequenting the local pub more often so her house was free most weekends. They'd never be able to come over to my house. My parents never left the house. And even if they did, who'd want to witness the media circus and emotional rollercoaster that came with spending an evening at the Macmillans'?

But regardless of the baggage that came with hanging out with me, here I was. At a party, with friends. My friends. And it was a perfect night. Huddled around the television, we watched Pink

Floyd concerts from 1974 and sipped a concoction of port, sherry, Russian vodka and lemonade, all stolen from parents' alcohol cabinets. Not mine. Mum didn't drink any more and Dad never left any alcohol behind. Our alcohol cabinet looked like a bargain shelf on Boxing Day – stripped clean and already caked in dust.

'Hey Izzy, you should wear your hair like that,' said Dougie, pointing to the punk-haired girl on the TV who wore her hair to one side to show off a collection of ear piercings.

'Yeah, definitely,' replied Izzy, gingerly tucking a wisp of hair behind her ear.

'I love her outfit too.' He took a long drag from his cigarette and exhaled, making smoke circles. 'Girls in that time really knew how to dress,' he added, gesturing towards the television set with a crystal brandy glass taken from Debbie's mum's 'Do Not Touch' dining room cabinet. Crystal never looked more at home than in Dougie s hand. He was the epitome of cool. I would have to take notes on his clothes tonight and what he said. Perhaps I could pass off one of his comments as if it was my own.

'So, Sam. What's your favourite Ramones album?' said Dougie, with a slight grin growing across his face.

Shit. It never crossed my mind to do some

research before sporting this shirt. 'Um... I like them all.' Good save. Or was it?

'I liked *Brain Drain*. Not as good as *Rocket to Russia* but "I Believe in Miracles" has become a classic,' spurted out Worm, who was randomly wearing a kitchen bowl on his head. I'd have to pick his brain later, if he wasn't too drunk.

'I'm bored,' announced Dougie. 'Let's play a game.'

'Spin the bottle?' eagerly asked Worm, taking the bowl off his head.

Izzy rolled her eyes. 'Pervert.'

'Beer Pong?' said Max.

'My mum will kill me if she found out I used her crystal wedding glasses to play Beer Pong. No way,' said Debbie.

'I've got it – "Never Have I Ever",' Dougie said, pushing the armchairs to the side. He sat on the floor with his legs folded in, everyone else taking his cue. I sat in the circle between Max and Debbie, and everyone looked around wondering who was going to go first.

'You start, Dougie. It was your idea,' Frankie finally said, sweeping her hair over one shoulder, trying to expose the hoop piercing on her ear, like the girl on the TV.

'OK, who hasn't played before?' he asked, looking at me.

Slowly I raised my hand, like I was sitting in class waiting for the teacher to call on me. Debbie rolled her eyes and tugged my arm down.

'Someone states something they've never done before and everyone who has done it has to take a drink. So, if I was to say, 'Never have I ever dyed my hair' then Debbie and Izzy would have to take a drink.'

'Worm would have to take a drink too then,' laughed Max.

'Hey! My hair is 100 per cent natural! With barely any dye!' Debbie yelled.

'OK, I think I get it,' I said.

'OK. Here we go. Never have I ever tried out for the under-16s football team and got laughed at.'

'Oh come on. I was 13! My dad made me!' said Max, taking a big swig of his brandy, Coke and schnapps concoction. 'Never have I ever cried in public when Take That split up.'

Izzy smiled, and downed the last of her sherry and lemonade. 'Very funny. My turn. Never have I ever had to change schools.' She looked at me from across the circle and smiled.

I smiled back and cautiously took a sip from my glass. Thick liquid burned my throat and warmed my belly. I didn't know what Worm had put in there. Gasoline? Fabric softener?

'More!' said Dougie.

I took another drink, this time a big gulp that filled my cheeks with searing-hot whisky and Dr Pepper. I coughed loudly, and my eyes watered. Clearing my throat, I said, 'Never have I ever… listened to a Ramones album.' I shrugged, throwing up my hands in public defeat.

Everyone laughed and took drinks. 'I knew it,' said Max, glancing at Dougie.

'Good for you, Sam. Who cares, yeah?' he said, shrugging his shoulders.

Worm sympathetically slapped me on the back, and Max clinked my glass. 'Who cares?' Everyone toasted their glasses to me, repeating, 'Who cares?'

At that moment, I felt a faint flutter of something I hadn't felt in a while. I was having fun tonight. I had made friends in the darkest of places, during the worst time in my life. I was happy, I think. I felt like anything was possible in that moment, that boundless infinite moment. I raised my glass to them and smiled, before finishing the glass. Worm and Max clapped. Izzy looked at me and smiled. And for a moment, I got lost in her golden-green eyes that shimmered in the lamplight she sat under.

'My turn,' announced Debbie. 'Never have I ever got drunk and thrown up in a bush.'

'You're supposed to say something you haven't done, Debs,' said Dougie, as everyone laughed.

'Oh. OK… never have I ever cheated in class.'

Worm and Max clinked their glasses, toasting to their achievement, and drank the last of their brandy, gin and Coke mixes. Slowly, I took a drink.

'You, Sam?' asked Debbie.

'Yeah, once.'

'What happened?' said Izzy, leaning in.

'I stole my brother's essay on Impressionism and tried to pass it off as my own to pass my GCSEs in Art Studies.' Charlie knew a lot about art. It interested him, spoke to him, inspired him. When we drifted apart, art became his friend, his family. His room became an empty canvas soon covered in asymmetrical brush strokes, swirls and heavy flicks in whatever colour he fancied that day. Dad never noticed and Mum wanted to repaint it cream, but he loved it. So did I. It was his passion. It was him. And no matter what I read about who he really was, his love of art was the one thing I could hold onto as being truthful, honest.

'Did you get caught?' she asked.

'Yes, by my brother. But he didn't tell anyone... He never would have told on me,' I said, feeling my forehead begin to ache. Why am I thinking about him? Why now, here? Please stop talking. Everyone, please stop talking.

'You must miss him every day,' she said. And just like that, I felt my shoulders relax. Just like that, I felt like it was only Izzy and I in this room.

Everyone else, everything else dissipated in the air around us. There was only us. Only the emotion that stirred within me remained with us.

Nodding, I suddenly felt her arms around me. She hugged me tightly and it was then that I realised that no one had ever acknowledged my brother's death. They talked of his actions, his troubles, the monsters inside his head. But they never talked about his death, or my family's loss. My brother was dead and he was never coming back. Yes, I mourned him. Yes, I missed him. And I was sick of being ashamed of that.

When Izzy pulled away, I saw Worm and Max looking at Dougie. When I looked too, I saw that his jaw was clenched and his eyes were dark. My cheeks started to flush and get warm. My welcome was fading, fast.

Dougie cleared his throat, gaining Izzy's attention. 'Never have I ever – '

' – Dougie, it's my turn,' said Worm, interrupting him.

'Never have I ever,' he continued, ignoring Worm, 'been called the school slut. How many people have you slept with now? Six? Seven? Ten?'

A sharp silence filled the air, as everyone stopped breathing. I looked around wondering who was going to take a drink. That's when I saw Izzy's face. Cheeks red, black-rimmed eyes watering, she glared at Dougie with a look that startled me. Was he talking about Izzy? My Izzy? Of course, she wasn't *my* Izzy.

'You're so hypocritical!' she yelled, standing up. Marching through the circle, she stormed out of the house letting the door slam wildly behind.

No one said anything at first, but then Dougie walked over and turned up the television. Loud drums and electric guitar filled the room once again, but all I heard was the deafening absence of Izzy. Too scared to look up and risk meeting Dougie's eyes, I hurried to the door. Cool air biting at my arms as I walked out into the night, I called after her, 'Izzy!'

I could see her further down the street, about to turn right around the corner. She ignored me and kept walking. The light from the full moon lit up the road around her, as if a spotlight followed her every move.

I jogged lightly and caught up to her within seconds. 'Izzy, are you OK?'

'Just go back to the house, Sam. I'm fine.' The moonlight illuminated the wetness that sparkled on her delicate cheekbones.

'You're not. You're crying.'

'No, I'm not – '

' – I know what crying looks like,' I said, reaching out a hand to her. She stopped and turned to face me. She was beautiful. But it wasn't a good time to tell her. 'I'm sorry you're upset.'

'I'm not upset at you,' she said, wiping tears from her chin.

'He's just drunk. We all are.'

She nodded, but didn't say anything. A part of me wanted to run back inside to check if Dougie was mad at me for being outside with her, for being alone with her, for thinking of things that involved her. But a bigger part of me wanted to stay right there with her all night. I knew it couldn't last forever. 'Are you going back inside?' I eventually asked.

'No, I should get home,' she said, patting her face as if she could press away the redness.

'Can I walk you home?'

'No, I'm not far. I'm actually just on the other side of the woodlands.'

'You sure I can't walk with you?'

I wanted to push some more, but she was already starting to turn away. She threw a hand up gently in the air, 'Goodnight, Sam. Thanks for… I don't know, but thanks.'

I watched her walk away, her hair bouncing up and down with each step. The strands glistened in the warm glow of the streetlights, and her ear piercing caught the amber sparks from overhead.

Before she disappeared into the darkness, she glanced back at me. Just once, but it was enough.

I went to bed that night still feeling her arms around me, and her chin on my shoulder. And for once, my dreams weren't filled with gunshots, blood and enlarged student photos on easels. For once, I dreamt of gardenia perfume and freshly shampooed hair. For the first time in months, I slept through the night.

Chapter 7

'Look on Down from the Bridge'
(Mazzy Star, Autumn 1996)

That night was never talked about again. Never again did we discuss the bitter words that slipped from Dougie's mouth and the tears that fell from Izzy's cheeks. We never acknowledged that she hugged me, or that I ran after her in the night, or that I would have gladly done both all over again. We just never talked about it.

A few weekend hangouts with Dougie and his friends soon turned into regular invites to their primary afterschool activity – coffee and conversation on the steps of the High Street Art Gallery. Occasionally they would meet up in the cafe and split baskets of chips and pints of Coke, but their afternoon staple tended to be the gallery steps.

At first, the notion of sitting on a cold step drinking passable blended coffee and discussing music and art seemed too foreign to me. Prior to Charlie's debut performance as the nation's psychopath, my afternoons after school were spent practising piano scales, finishing homework or sobering Dad up before Mum got home from work. The idea that people had that much time to dedicate to simply talking seemed so frivolous, and if I'm honest, possibly even selfish.

But they talked. And talked. And when conversation began to dry up and High Street shoppers started to head home, Dougie stood up, thanked everyone for their thoughts and started walking home, and we followed. Most afternoons they met on those steps and most afternoons I learned the most amazing things that I wouldn't have known otherwise. I hadn't realised how small my immediate world had been before these people.

It was through conversations about Kevin Carter and Larry Clark that I discovered Dougie's passion for photography. I had previously pegged him as a tortured musician, perhaps bass guitar, but apparently his interest lay with lenses, composition and shutter speeds. I learned that Izzy grew up horse-riding and could speak French. Although she openly debated William Faulkner, she occasionally expressed a much-harboured love of Roald Dahl books. I found out that Worm's real name was James and that his nickname came from an incident involving the accidental ingestion of an earthworm when he was nine years old. Max's discussions focused on music mostly, but there were occasionally times when he spoke of team sports, such as the latest Real Madrid scores. It was at that time that his friends stared at him, as if he had just grown two heads. So he quickly turned the conversation back to music.

In Debbie's case, conversation steered towards her 'pet peeve of the week' whether it was manufactured girl bands, Dolly the cloned sheep or too-tight jam jar lids. Generally everything tended to annoy Debbie at some point in her life. Even Izzy herself. It turned out Izzy and Debbie were former enemies, having spent most of the early academy years mocking each other. Izzy and her former friends, 'plastic Barbies' as Debbie called them, made fun of Dougie and his friends' love of indie rock and vintage T-shirts. Debbie was repulsed by Izzy's too-short skirts and too-tight tops that gained her attention from almost every male in the building, including the teachers. But yet here they were sitting side by side, sipping coffee and sharing stories as if they'd always been friends. I think that was what I loved most about these people that I'd started spending all my free time with – they were accepting. Regardless of background and an unshared past, they offered you a place without condition or question.

Sitting on the bus on the way back to Pembrook, I didn't replay Dougie's debate of whether there was still a place in society for a monarchy. I didn't remember Debbie's ridiculous impression of Margaret Thatcher, or even the taste of the bittersweet coffee that burned my tongue as I laughed at Worm's story. Only one thought kept me company on the bus ride home. Only one thought occupied my mind as I edged up the driveway, and that was Izzy. I thought about the way her dark eyelashes curl out and up away from her green eyes that have flecks of gold, and how she bites down on her bottom lip when she's engaged in a discussion.

Walking up to the front door, I instinctively glanced around feeling eyes burning into my back. Across the street, a tall shadow moved in front of the window. I could see fingers curl around the curtains and prying eyes dart across the street towards me. 'Hi, Mrs Cooper,' I called out, giving her an exaggerated wave. The curtains snapped closed and the shadow quickly moved away.

Turning back to the door, I could hear the vibrations through the wood as my parents' voices got louder. Their day was either spent screaming at each other or ignoring each other. There was no middle ground for them, not any more. Every day I was as much in the dark about their marital status as they were. Taking a deep breath, I pushed down on the door handle and stepped inside.

'So is this your plan? Erase all memories of our son and just pretend that he never existed?'

'We need to sell the house and it's not going to sell with all of his stuff here! No one wants to be reminded of him,' said my dad.

'That's not the reason why the house isn't selling, and you know it. It's nothing to do with his stuff. It's just stuff! And it's *you* that doesn't want to be reminded of him!'

'Fine, I don't want to be reminded of him! Is that what you want to hear? Do you want me to say that I'd rather just forget him? Do you want me to say that I wish he was never born?'

'Don't say that,' sobbed my mum.

I stood in the kitchen, invisible to them, listening to them battle and blame each other. When they didn't notice me or feel my presence, I turned and went upstairs. When would they realise that screaming at each other wouldn't bring Charlie back? And my dad didn't mean those things. Of course, he didn't want to forget him. Of course, he wished he had been born. Right?

At the top of the stairs sat a small stack of cardboard boxes. Written on the sides in black permanent marker was my brother's name. I glanced back down but knew they'd be at it for ages, so I slowly lifted the lid off the first box. A faint musty smell escaped from inside. Letting the lid hit the carpeted floor gently, I allowed my hand to explore the contents. Old textbooks, a ceramic craft dated 1985 with the heading 'Happy Father's Day' and studded football shoes, unstained with grass. Dad always pushed Charlie towards sports, but he always found a way back to his art.

Sliding the lid back on, I stroked my hand across the remaining boxes and wondered how many memories of Charlie would be lost if these were thrown out. Both of my parents were right – we couldn't sell the house with Charlie's stuff still here but we also couldn't erase him either.

Knocking the lid off another box, I was at first disappointed to find solely paperwork but at second glance I realised that the papers were Charlie's old school reports. Placing a large stack on my lap, I leaned against the wall and began looking through them. Some dated back to nursery school, where a 'school report' was a single paragraph on a piece of yellow card dotted with smiley faces. Words such as creative, playful and energetic dominated the initial reports. But as he got older and entered the academy, the reports painted a very different picture of my brother: *'daydreamer; shy; quiet; very bright; doesn't appear to find the work challenging enough; bored; discouraged; withdrawn; doesn't sustain eye contact; often fidgets in class; has trouble making friends; sometimes lies to adults and peers; seems distracted.*' What happened to the creative, playful and energetic little boy? What happened to my brother?

The next morning, we started the day like any other normal family not impacted by national scandal. We drove around the neighbouring towns, scoped out a few properties in Knightsbridge and contemplated what areas we wanted to start a new life in. But every time we got close to making an offer the sellers would discover our identity and decline a sale. By the time we returned to Pembrook, pulling up to the old stone driveway, the 'House for Sale' sign in the front garden had been defaced to now read 'Satan's House'. I wondered if we would ever be able to sell the house. The agent certainly had her work cut out for her, trying to sell the home that the town sociopath grew up in, where he plotted his massacre, selected his victims, chose his weapons. The truth was we would never have returned to this house in the beginning, but we had nowhere else to go. Every relative within a fifty-mile radius turned their backs on us. The only relative who still took our calls was my mum's sister Jackie, but she lived way down south. Everyone else quickly distanced themselves from my family, afraid the blood of guilt would stain their hands too.

I contemplated removing the dirt from the sign, but decided that it best represented how I felt just as it was. 'I'm going for a walk,' I shouted out into the kitchen. Even though I got no answer, I heard the temporary pause of closing drawers from Charlie's room, so I knew Mum heard me. Ever since the police had turned his bedroom upside down looking for evidence of a motive, Mum had spent almost every day putting it back together exactly the way Charlie had it before. Every day, something didn't look right to her – a book was on the wrong shelf, a shirt was in the wrong drawer, his blue socks should be on the floor by the laundry basket, not in the basket. Every day she thought she remembered one more detail about the layout of his room, but by the next day she was back to moving stuff around. To her, it would never be perfect.

Once I got down the street, I rounded the brick wall and stepped onto the path that snaked all the way around the other streets to the small park near Bristol Lane. Rain puddles dotted along the path, leading the way. I thought I heard voices ahead of me, but when I got to the park, it was void of laughing children on swings and teenagers kicking a football in the neighbouring field. In fact, it was practically empty. All but one of the swings at the end of the park were vacant. And when I walked nearer, intending to glance briefly before walking on with my head down, I noticed a familiar figure slumped against the chains of the swing. His face was thin, covered in grey-speckled stubble, and his eyes were outlined in dark-purple bags. At first, I wanted to quickly turn around and run back to the house, but I knew that it would be my only opportunity to say anything if anything was to be said. And something needed to be said. My belly churned and fluttered wildly.

'Hello, Mr Allans,' I muttered with apprehensiveness.

He looked up, and I could see that behind his tortured expression he was, in a strange way, glad to see me. He motioned to the empty swing next to him, and I sat quickly before he changed his mind.

'How are you doing, Sam?' he asked, gravely.

'We're...' I didn't know that to say. We're fine? We're surviving? The truth was, we were neither. So, I shrugged.

'I was sorry you were asked not to come back to Pembrook.'

'Have you gone back yet?' I asked.

'I decided to take a year off,' he mumbled,

looking down at his shoes as they sat in a thin veil of water under the swing. 'How's the new school?'

'It's OK, I guess. Probably won't last the year, to be honest. Word spreads far, you know.' I kicked at a stone on the ground below me, rolling it under the sole of my shoe.

'I see your house is up for sale?'

'Yeah, that's not going so well. Not a lot of interest, you know?'

'It'll take time. People need time.'

'Do you?' I asked cautiously.

'Honestly, I don't know what I need. Everything's changed,' he said, his voice cracking at the end. He gripped the swing chains tighter. I could hear a faint squeaking from his mouth as he desperately tried to suppress a cry.

In the distance, I could hear dogs barking as the train passed by the houses behind us. The wheels dragged along the metal tracks as the engine slowed down. It would be stopping at Pembrook Station soon, where commuters would be getting off and teenagers would be getting on, desperate to get out of town even for a few hours. Even long before the shootings, people were desperate to leave Pembrook. Nobody chose to stay. Nobody chose to spend their life here. The people who stayed behind were either too scared to leave or too stupid to avoid getting stuck. I knew why my parents stayed. They were the ones stupid enough to get stuck. My mum got pregnant with Charlie when she was seventeen and my dad was nineteen. Before that, she'd planned on going to university in London. She wanted to be a writer. She wanted to change people's lives with her stories. Now she was just desperate to be heard in her own home. Maybe Dad was right. If Charlie had never been born, my mum might have become a successful writer, she might have been happy, and fourteen lives might have been saved.

'I should probably be getting back,' I eventually said, getting up from the swing.

'I'm sorry, Sam. You don't need to hear this. You know better than anyone how much has changed.'

'Did you think he was going to shoot you too?' I blurted out suddenly.

He stared at me for a moment, then his eyes glazed over again. 'No. I saw his face when he passed by the art room. He looked in, looked right at me. Or maybe even right through me. But I knew he wasn't going to shoot me.'

'He always said you were his favourite teacher. He loved art because of you.' I started to walk away, feeling like something else was still unsaid.

'Sam?' I turned around and saw Mr Allans standing in front of the swing. His body swayed slightly, like he was drunk. 'I'm sorry I couldn't help him.'

I shook my head. 'I think it's me that should be saying sorry to you.'

'For what?'

'I don't know yet. For everything. For nothing. I honestly don't know, but I thought someone in my family should say it.' I still remember the look on his face before I walked away. I couldn't read his expression, and maybe he intended for me not to.

Seeing him consumed the rest of my day. His expression, his appearance, his grief was all I could think about. No matter how far I walked, how loud I blasted my music in my bedroom, how many hours of TV I subjected my brain to, I could not get past that meeting in the park.

A sharp pain occupied my head, pressing in from my temples. The medication bottle that Dr Albreck had prescribed loomed over me from up on the shelf, but I resisted its temptation. I didn't want to feel numb or forget. Seeing Mr Allans reminded me that I wasn't allowed to be excused from this. The guilt I felt every day needed to be felt. It was my punishment. I finally lay down on my bed, the cool pillow soothing my burning cheeks. Before I drifted off, I saw Charlie standing before me. Wearing jeans, black trainers and a hooded sweatshirt with paint splotches on the sleeves. His eyes were dark, harbouring secrets behind them, but he smiled at me. He slid his hands into his pockets and nodded gently, as if he was acknowledging my pain. But when I blinked, he was gone and I was alone again, left with the memories of that morning.

The day it happened would have started off like any other day, if my alarm had gone off. But it didn't. I must have forgotten to set it. Whatever the reason, I slept right through until 8.25am. By the time I had raced out of the shower, my mum had already left for work. I could hear Dad's snoring from the spare bedroom. I noticed my brother's backpack was gone from the kitchen counter. He left before I had a chance to say goodbye. But at that time, I didn't care. I thought I would see him in the corridors at school, or at least at the dinner table that evening. But I didn't see him at school that day. I was late. Mum forgot to make my lunch that morning, so I took time to shove a messy ham sandwich into a brown paper bag along with a browning banana. I didn't arrive at school until 9.08am.

I knew something was strange about that morning the moment I turned onto Pembrook Road. A cluster of people had gathered on the street, about halfway down, and when I got closer I realised that they could go no further. A blue barricade stood between them and Pembrook

Academy, and beside it a line of police officers. At first, I was curious and actually happy. I thought maybe there had been an electricity fault or a gas leak, and that they were shutting down the school for the day. And I was right, the school had been closed, but for a very different reason. That reason would change my life forever, and this town.

We didn't know anything until that evening. The news confirmed what the police and school officials had told us, that my brother Charlie had been a victim of a devastating school incident. We grieved for him. And that night would be the first and last time that we would ever comfort each other, like a normal family would. Even my dad mourned with us, holding my mum tighter than I had ever seen him do. But by the next day, when the truth hit us like a speeding train, a distance grew between us all that was so deep that it could never be repaired. We broke.

They say the truth sets you free. It didn't. It destroyed us.

Chapter 8

'When You're Gone' *(Cranberries, Autumn 1996)*

The next day at school, I waited for everyone in the school car park, in front of the football field. After facing Mr Allans, I really needed to see everyone, to feel included in something. I needed people around to help distract me from the darkness looming inside, waiting to take over. But by 3.15pm, no one had arrived.

An uneasy ache started building in my stomach as I found myself searching the field and the car park for Dougie, Izzy, anyone. But the only noises I heard were the engine roars of the buses and the mundane chatter of teenagers heading home. Even if the absence of the group that I called my friends was an indication of what was to come, I could never go back to that mundane chatter. I had already evolved past it.

Dougie had opened up a world of curiosity for me, and I was never going back. Gone were the days of craving silent family dinners and solitary evenings in my bedroom listening to Bach. These had been replaced with a growing interest in heated debates about music, pop culture, the media, art, warfare, literature, even science. Dougie brought out a side in me that I didn't know existed – a need for more. Not necessarily to learn more or know more, but a desire to have more in my life. More laughter, more freedom of speech, more memories. For once in my life, I was acting my age. I was listening to loud music, drinking alcohol, crushing on a girl that I'd never get. For once, I had a social life, one that appropriately conflicted with my homework assignments, like a typical teenager. For once, the normality I sought was within arm's reach.

Perhaps if my brother had experienced this, he wouldn't have felt so alone and isolated from the world outside. Perhaps if he'd socialised more, opened himself up to alternative means of living then he wouldn't have felt stuck in the cycle of sleeping, school, chores; sleeping, school, chores. He wouldn't have felt stuck in Pembrook, like Mum and Dad.

At 3.45pm, I started to walk away from the field back towards the bus stop that would take me back to the haunted town of Pembrook.

'Sam!'

I spun around and saw Izzy in the doorway of the assembly hall. I jogged to reach her but slowed to a more casual walk as I got closer. 'Hey.'

'Have you been waiting long? I got stuck chatting to Ms Sheffer after History,' she said, letting the exit door close and lock behind her. Ever since June, all of the schools had to install automatic locks on the doors so the only entrance into the school from the outside was through the main office. Students and staff had to wear ID tags, and those without had to sign in at the office and get a visitor's tag. Even students that arrived late had to enter in through the office. Students weren't just students any more. We were all potential threats to schools now, any of us possibly harbouring a desire to bring a gun to school.

'Where is everyone?' I asked.

'Dougie skipped school today, Worm is grounded this week after he came home drunk on Friday night and threw up in his mum's vase. Max has to help his dad out at the shop and Debbie has a dentist appointment.'

'Oh, so we're not going to the gallery?' I said, feeling a pit in my stomach. It was the only thing I looked forward to these days.

'We can still go, if you like?'

I cleared my throat and attempted to contain the excitement that was bubbling within me, even though I wanted to scream at the top of my lungs. 'Sure, whatever.'

When we got to the coffee shop in the basement of the gallery, I ordered two milky coffees, one with sugar. Blowing on the frothy coffee until it cooled, we walked back outside and positioned ourselves on the middle row of the steps. Lifting the cup to my lips, I winced as the hot coffee burned my tongue.

'Hot? Yeah, mine too. Coffee sucks here.'

'I thought I was the only one that thought that,' I grinned.

'I don't know who decided the coffee here was the best. And the steps are so uncomfortable. And, just wait till it snows. That's even more fun.'

'Have you ever been inside?'

She nodded, 'Once, with my mum. They have a great exhibition on in January, actually.'

I nodded in agreement, although having no idea what was happening in January but I would check when I got home. I glanced up and saw her playing with the plastic flap on the coffee cup lid. Bending it back and forth, the plastic eventually whitened and broke off. Was she nervous too?

'So, I'm glad we got a chance to hang out just the two of us,' she said, slowly looking up at me.

'Really?' I asked.

'Yeah, I wanted to let you know that I'm sorry

for what's going on with you. I didn't want to say anything in front of anyone else. I can't imagine how hard this has all been.'

'Thanks.' I didn't know what else to say. I knew by the way she inched off the step and fidgeted with the straps of her schoolbag that she wanted to ask me more, or say more. So I waited. I could smell the floral scent of her perfume or shampoo, and resisted leaning in closer. I wondered if she knew how I felt about her. She must. I wasn't very good at pretending. Not like my brother, I guess.

Eventually she cleared her throat, and flicked away a piece of hair that fell across her eyes. 'Did you know?'

'What he had planned? No, of course not.'

'Sorry, stupid question.' She sipped on her coffee, lightly blowing on the frothy top. Her eyes gazed out at the bustling street in front of us. Double-decker buses, black cabs and the occasional work van zipped around the lanes of traffic. A slight breeze lifted the ends of her hair around her face, but she didn't try to smooth them down. She just let them rise and coil in the gentle wind, landing wherever they pleased. Eventually her eyes found mine again. 'You really had no idea?'

I shook my head, and focused my gaze down on my toes that twitched and curled in my trainers. 'How could I? He didn't really talk to me about how he was feeling. I didn't know he was depressed, suicidal, and whatever else the papers say he was. He was just Charlie my brother. He wasn't this person. I don't recognise the boy they depict on the news. I've never met *him* before. The Charlie I knew was funny and kind, and took care of me. He wasn't a monster.' I was surprised by how easy it was to talk to Izzy about this. The words poured out effortlessly, as if they lived beneath my tongue waiting to spill out at the first question asked. Yet, they disappeared in Dr Albreck's office and were nowhere to be found when I looked at Mum and Dad. I could have talked to Izzy all night.

She leaned in and placed a hand on my forearm, squeezing gently. 'You know the real Charlie, and that's all that counts.'

'Is it? Wouldn't it be better, more honest, to know the Charlie that killed fourteen people? Otherwise, the person I knew is nothing but a myth. An illusion.'

'Sam, you're allowed to grieve. You lost someone on that day too. Just remember that. You don't need to spend this year investigating him. You're allowed to just mourn him.'

'I can't. How can I grieve for someone I didn't really know?'

She leaned back against the step ledge behind her. As she swirled the contents of her coffee cup, letting some spill out of the open hole in the lid, her eyes wandered out onto the street and fixed on something beyond the shoppers and tall brick buildings.

'Anyway, enough about my messed-up life. Tell me about yours?' I asked.

'I think we're very similar, Sam,' she said, her eyes still set on the street.

'Oh, did you have a brother that took a gun to school then turned it on himself?'

'No,' she smiled, gazing back towards me. 'I mean, you feel invisible yet with a spotlight on you at all times. I feel the same.'

'Are you close to your parents?'

'I was but after my mum died and my dad started dating Carol, it was like I didn't exist any more. With my mum, we were a family. But with Carol, it's like he's starting a whole new family without me.'

'Have you tried to talk to him about how you feel?'

'Have you tried talking to your parents about how you feel?'

'Point taken.'

'Besides, he would just think I was acting up again. He knows I hate Carol and she hates me. And I don't blame her. I was a real bitch in the beginning. Who am I kidding? I'm still a bitch. No one can replace my mum, you know? When she first moved in, I started hanging out with an older group, drinking, staying out late, going to parties. I started seeing this older guy. I was trying to get my dad's attention, but it never seemed to work so I kept upping the ante.'

'Is that why you started seeing Dougie?'

She looked at me, her eyes fluttering fast.

'I'm sorry. I didn't mean – '

' – It's fine. I know what you mean – tattoos, piercings, punk rock. My dad hates Dougie. But he's like a magnet, you know. Everyone is just drawn to him.'

I knew exactly what she meant. I was drawn to him. I even wanted to be him. But then again, I wanted to be anyone but me right now. 'Thank you,' I said quietly.

'What for?'

'For everything – for not judging me, for not ignoring me. People aren't exactly welcoming me and my family. But I understand. We probably deserve that.'

'You don't need to thank me, Sam, or anyone else. You don't give yourself nearly enough credit.' She reached out and rested a hand on my arm again, but didn't squeeze it sympathetically this time. This time she left it there, and leaned in.

Izzy's eyes burned into mine and I realised

that soft amber flecks on the outside surrounded the green I was used to seeing. Cheeks suddenly going pink, Izzy turned away from me and started gathering the straps of her backpack. 'I better get going. Carol is cooking her famous Beef Wellington tonight and Dad will go spare if I'm not home soon. You know, I think I'm going vegetarian. I can't wait to tell them when I get home. I'll wait until after she's finished cooking. See you later, Sam.'

Izzy bounded down the steps, glancing around once before she crossed the road and disappeared around the corner of Potter Avenue. Unlike her, I wasn't expected at home. And unlike her, a family dinner wasn't waiting for me regardless of how forced it was. So, I hung out on the gallery steps until the sun set deep into the skyline beyond the office buildings.

The streets seemed to come alive in the early evening. Noises bounced off the buildings and windows, and swirled around me. The sounds were comforting. But when I got home, the only sounds I heard were my dad's radio in the garage, and my mum's muffled but distinct sobbing from her bedroom. Those sounds weren't comforting. Those sounds threatened to drown me.

Chapter 9

'No Place to Hide' *(Korn, Autumn 1996)*

That Saturday, I awoke to a thumping sound from the hallway. Dragging a hoodie up from the floor beneath the bed frame, I pulled it over my head. Swinging one leg at a time over the bed, I let my feet hit the ground hard. Rubbing my hands over my face, I took a deep breath. Another day to get through. Another day of new headlines, new revelations, new disappointments. When would the papers move on to another story?

Staggering downstairs, I found the source of the thumping. A pile of letters and newspapers lay under the letterbox untouched. Gathering them up in my arms, I cradled them through into the kitchen and let them spill out across the counter. As the bills and junk mail slithered over the smooth granite, I saw my brother's face looking back at me. Here we go. Grabbing the newspaper, I brought it up to my face so my eyes were level with his, even though I didn't recognise the image staring back at me any more.

They had found him, the man who'd got a gun for my brother. They'd finally tracked him down and arrested him. Inset was a small slightly fuzzy CCTV image of the man meeting my brother outside a retail park a little after 1am the week before the shootings. I didn't recognise the man, but I knew my brother and that was him. What was he doing out at 1am? Why didn't we know about this 1am meeting? My bedroom was right down the hall from Charlie's. My parents' was beside his. Were we that oblivious to each other's whereabouts?

Charlie barely looked like himself in the photo – dark hoodie pulled up, quite similar to mine, black jogging bottoms loose at the waist, also like mine. Looking down at my own clothing and the image in the CCTV footage, it hit me that perhaps we weren't so different. Bile rose up in my throat as the image stared back at me, taunting me. I suddenly threw the paper across the counter, hearing it hit the floor on the other side, and ripped off my hoodie, exposing the red T-shirt underneath. We were different. We had to be.

But curiosity burned into me as usual, and I crept through to the living room. Turning on the news, I saw a bigger image of the man arrested. His name was Greg and he was older than Charlie, in his late thirties. An employed electrician. Married. One kid. An arms dealer on the side. His 'special talent' was acquiring non-licensed 9mm pistols and Smith & Wesson Magnum revolvers for anyone with cash, no questions asked. I wondered if Charlie hadn't been able to get an unlicensed handgun from this guy, if he would have turned to someone else or if he would have given up, maybe even finally asked for help. That's something I'd never know.

After that, BBC reporters and psychology professors – self-acclaimed 'experts' – occupied the remaining news headlines with comparisons between my brother and the 1987 mass shooter, Robert Hurd, who'd killed sixteen people over the course of one afternoon. Both were male. Both were in the '18-27 years' age bracket. Both enjoyed violent movies and videogames. Both were considered to be 'loners' by neighbours and school classmates. But it was the last item on the 'checklist' that made me sit up. Both were medically diagnosed as depressed – posthumously, of course. There it was – profile and motive decided.

I was engrossed, leaning in for every word spoken. Mrs Bell had finally passed away, having spent weeks in the intensive care unit at St John's Hospital. Apparently she had been battling a staph infection from a gunshot wound. But the psychologists' reports and her death weren't the primary headlines for that day. There was also a petition circling around towns neighbouring Pembrook that was fast gaining signatures and was predicted to soon spread to the surrounding cities and eventually through the country. The petition called for a total ban on all handguns across the entire United Kingdom. It even had a name – the Pembrook Petition. Thirteen thousand people had already put their names to it. A pretty redheaded reporter with shiny pink lipstick was asking a local policeman to speculate whether this new petition would result in a change in the law, and if so, whether it would deter future 'depressed persons' from committing acts similar to that at Pembrook Academy. The policeman was evidently unsure how to answer this and after clearing his throat several times to buy himself more response time, he finally answered, 'Possibly.'

When asked if Charlie had been 'aided by an accomplice', Chief Inspector Morrison confirmed that several conversations had occurred between them and Adam Webster, Charlie's 'best friend', but it was determined that my brother acted alone. Adam was no friend of my brother, especially not a 'best friend'. Not that I had much experience before Dougie and Izzy entered my messed-up life, but my understanding was that a best friend was someone who attended their friend's funeral, who sent their condolences to his family, who reached out to struggling family members.

When probed for more details about the morning of the shooting, the chief inspector said that a new witness had come forward attesting to hearing Charlie shout, 'I'm the law!' before he opened fire in the assembly hall. However, another student had refuted that claim, instead affirming the original account from a student that my brother didn't say anything before pulling the trigger. One student claimed to have heard him crying, whilst another swore that she heard him laughing.

I was no closer to the truth now than I was five months previously. Everyone claimed to have another piece of the puzzle, yet nothing fitted the way it should. Nothing was making sense to me.

The report ended with the most alarming claim of them all, that my brother entered that building in June having a concoction of drugs in his system, ranging from Adderall to Prozac to Speed. Someone even avowed to have seen him take Ecstasy at a school dance just the month before. Of course, no further comments would be made in the meantime, an intention that would probably last five minutes. Everyone loves to comment on a scandal, especially one that was fast gaining international media attention.

With a dramatic flick of her red hair, the reporter moved on to a story about the Stone of Scone being returned to Edinburgh Castle after 700 years, and I turned the TV off. Fingers trembling wildly, I dropped the remote, hearing it hit the floor beside my slippers. Drugs. Adderall. Prozac. Speed. Ecstasy.

'What was that?' My dad charged into the living room. 'Sam, you're going to end up breaking that remote,' he said, snapping it up from the floor.

I glared at him – God forbid I damage his only source of interaction with the outside world. 'Dad, was Charlie on drugs?'

My dad stopped moving, freezing as if a cold blast of nitrogen had hit him. 'Where did you get that from?' he finally said.

'That's what they're saying on the news now. Was he? Did you ever find drugs in his room or in his bag, or what? Did he come home from a school dance high on Ecstasy?'

'Sam, the media is going to report whatever they want. I'm tired of having to defend this family all the time.' He continued walking over to the sofa and collapsed into the soft fabric, swinging his legs up onto the coffee table. A thin veil of sawdust and woodchips from the garage floor still remained on the soles of his slippers.

'Defend us? You didn't even make a statement to

the public after it happened! I've barely seen you since the shooting. Dad, you've been completely absent this entire time.'

'I've been dealing with this!' said my dad, rising to his feet again.

'How? By locking yourself in the garage? If that's dealing with this then yes, you get an 'A+' in handling difficult situations!'

'Watch your tone!'

'Or what, you're going to ground me? Great, do it! At least then you'd have to acknowledge me!'

My dad ignored me and turned the TV back on, raising the volume one notch at a time.

'Well, ground me!' I said, standing in front of him.

'Keep your voice down. If your mum hears you, she'll be in a state for the rest of the day.'

'Ground me, I'm asking you to. Please!'

My dad flung the remote beside him on the sofa and stood up. I'd forgotten how tall and broad he was, and for a moment I wondered if Charlie would have adopted his frame when he got a little older. His chest heaved in and out as he glared at me. But his expression broke, and his eyes darted to the floor as he shuffled back into the garage.

'Dad?'

But he never turned back, not even one final

glance to see me still standing there with my arms stretched out, waiting. Always waiting.

The weekend came and went, its presence another reminder of the absence of my brother. By Monday afternoon, I was back in Dr Albreck's waiting room but I wasn't waiting for her. Her waiting room splintered out into several small spaces, one being her office and another being Dr Fraser's – my new counsellor. Unlike her, he didn't keep to appointment times so by the time he called out my name I'd already scanned through three psychology journals and a copy of *Home and Garden.*

His office was the complete opposite of Dr Albreck's – messy, unorganised and with a dying potted plant in the corner. I didn't know what was more concerning to me, that he was 25 minutes late, that he looked like he'd already lost my case file in the mountain of paperwork on his desk, or that he was apparently completely incapable of keeping a plant alive.

'Sorry for the wait, Samuel,' he said, motioning for me to sit down on the red armchair beside him. Up close, he seemed older than I'd originally thought. Bushy brows dotted with thick greys, a receding hairline and crow's feet put him in the '45-55 years' age bracket. He wore the cliché uniform of someone trying too hard to appeal to the younger generation as if to say, 'Hey, I'm just like you. Let's talk.' He crossed his legs, his Converse briefly touching my shin. In Dr Albreck's office, our chairs sat opposite each other and with a huge coffee table between us. Here, we were close. Too close.

'So, Samuel, my name is Dr Fraser but I'd like for you to call me Alistair because here we're equals.'

Cringing inside, I resisted looking at my watch – how long had I been here? As long as he didn't refer to us as 'friends', I'd be fine. Swallowing hard, I said, 'It's nice to meet you,' even though I didn't really mean it but because it was expected after someone introduces himself.

'No need for formalities. I want you to feel comfortable.'

'OK.'

'So, tell me a little bit about yourself.'

'Don't you have my file? I can get it for you?' I said, getting up. I seemed to be looking for any reason to leave, even if just for a few minutes. Perhaps I could stall in getting my file and most of my session would be done. I would make sure to go to the bathroom too.

'Yes, I have your file on my desk,' he smiled. 'But I don't think a person should be defined by the words written in a case file. I want to hear something about you, from you. What do you think?'

I slumped back into the chair. I guess I was going to have to talk about myself after all. Maybe this would be the person to make me finally talk about what happened. Maybe this would work out after all. 'What do you want to know?'

'How do you spend your free time? Do you have any hobbies?'

'Hobbies? Well, I used to play the piano. And very recently I started experimenting with social interactions.'

'You mean, making friends?'

'Yes, I made some new friends.' I resisted the urge to smile, although saying those words made me want to. I had made friends. I could feel the corners of my mouth going upwards involuntarily.

'I can see that makes you happy. Sam, I want you to think of us as friends too.'

My smile started to fade. Did he just say the word 'friends'?

He went on, 'Here, we're just two friends catching up.'

And there it was again. 'Friends.' I could see where this was going. With that I stood up. 'Dr Fraser, thank you for your time. I don't really see this as working out. But I would like to offer you tips that I just learned from *Home and Garden* that I read in the waiting room while I sat waiting for almost a half hour: a spot near a south-facing window, a pebble tray for extra humidity and consistent watering,' I said, pointing to the browning plant in the corner.

When I turned back to close the door, I saw 'Alistair' still sitting there in his burgundy armchair with his mouth agape. The next day, I rang the office and requested another appointment with Dr Albreck. It would be different this time. This time I would make myself open up to her. I had to. This was my last shot. If this didn't work, nothing would help me out of this nightmare. Nothing would save me from this life.

Chapter 10

'Swallowed' *(Bush, Autumn 1996)*

I had another nightmare last night. I keep having the same one. At least I think it was the same one, but I can't tell. I have so many now, they all seem familiar. Too familiar. Anyway, in this dream we were together outside at the park near our house. He was saying something that I wouldn't comprehend after, a series of unfinished sentences and misused words. But in the dream, I understood him. I understood every word from his lips. Then he started running. I ran with him and when I asked him why we were running, he said people were chasing him. But when I looked behind us, all I saw was him. He was running away from himself.

And when I opened my eyelids, the vast emptiness that settled into me like a cold unfamiliar blanket reminded me that I had already dreamt this dream before.

I rolled over, pressing my face into the pillow

and screamed softly into the fabric. I hoisted myself onto my elbows and stared out of the window. The sky was unusually bright, and the clouds seemed separate as if one could exist without the other.

A click startled me and when I rolled back over I saw my dad standing in the doorway. Had he heard me scream? Had he too had a bad dream?

'Your mum wants to go to the post office.'

'OK,' I replied, wriggling my feet back inside the quilt.

'She can't go to town, so she's going to go to the one in Knightsbridge.'

'OK.'

My dad rolled his eyes, and sighed, 'So get up out of bed and go with her.'

'Why?'

'She doesn't want to go by herself.'

I stared at my dad wondering if the thought had entered his mind. 'So why don't *you* go with her?'

'You know Knightsbridge better than I do,' he shrugged.

'I go to school there. I'm not the town representative. I don't know where the post office is.'

'So get up, get dressed and go find it with her.' He slammed the door shut, leaving my body twisted in the bed covers.

Dragging my body out of the lukewarm shower

and down the stairs, I realised my mum was already waiting out in the car. When I stepped outside, I saw her huddled in the driver's seat with both hands on the steering wheel. She stared straight ahead, her eyes fixed on something that I would never know, never comprehend. Like my dream.

When we pulled up to the main carpark, I immediately noticed the large brown brick post office building across the road, which shared its space with the local bank. Mum hadn't seemed to notice it, or even to be looking for it, but I pointed it out as it sat next to the Red Cross shop. She nodded slowly.

'Why are we here anyway? Do you need to post something?' I asked, even just to fill the quiet space between us.

'Your father thought it was a stupid idea, but I want to try and get the mail stopped. I can't take much more of the kinds of post coming in. Nobody has anything nice to say.'

I opened my mouth to respond, but quickly closed it. Perhaps she didn't want to hear the truth. 'I don't know if they can do much from here. We should have gone into town.'

'I tried the town post office first, but they... weren't very sympathetic.'

We got out of the car, and crossed the street together. We didn't walk beside each other or try to interact once outside of the car, but we were there, together somewhat. I noticed she walked with her head down, and her eyes on the pavement beneath her. She didn't dare look up or face anyone. I wondered if people instantly recognised us from the newspapers or if it took them some time to place us.

As she queued up at the post office kiosks, I wandered around the shop floor. Giftcards, stationery gifts, sweets, bottled juices and, right by the cashier, a stack of newly printed newspapers with Charlie's silhouette captured. Above the pictures lay the words printed in charcoal grey – 'Charles Macmillan: A glimpse into his dark world.'

Then I did something I swore never to do. I bought it. I took out my wallet and paid 50p for a glimpse into my brother's dark world. Thankfully the girl behind the cash register didn't recognise me, so I was free to read all my brother's morbidly dark details in secret. I rolled up the newspaper and tucked it behind my back, into the hem of my jeans.

A familiar laugh jerked my head up, and through the cloudy window I saw Izzy's face. I saw her smile, her eyes, her flick of the hair. Leaning against the post office window, she giggled with a girl from school that I didn't know. Then she held up her hand, waved and started to walk away.

Shuffling clumsily through the Saturday midday crowd, I found my mum still in the queue. 'Mum, are you OK if I look around the town centre a bit before we head back? I have to get a few things.'

'Oh, want me to go with you?' she asked, with a desperately hopeful look in her eyes that I hated to crush.

'Actually, I'm just going to go myself. Do you mind if we meet back at the car in an hour?'

'Of course not,' she smiled. 'I don't have anywhere to be today.' Her smile faded from her lips.

I didn't stay to comfort her, or wait for her to be finished so she wasn't alone. I left her standing in the queue with a sample of hate mail in her arms to show the post office manager.

Swinging the doors wildly open, I narrowly missed knocking over an elderly man with a cane and a dog. I jogged lightly to the end of the street and faced a junction that divided into four sub-streets. I had only been at Knightsbridge for a couple of months, but I knew the street ahead would take me to High Street where the art gallery was, and the street on my right would take me to the academy and the fields.

Crossing over, I dodged light weekend traffic and picked up my pace as I headed for the art gallery.

I came to another break in the road. And there she was. Standing at the pedestrian crossing, waiting for the light to flash, with her hair slightly blowing in the wind. Suddenly I wasn't sure if I wanted her to turn around. What would I say? What would she want to say to me?

'Sam?'

Except she did turn around and now she was staring at me, waiting.

'Oh hey, I didn't see you there,' I lied.

The light behind her flashed but she walked away from the crossing, closer to me. She held up her hands. 'What are you doing here?'

'I was in town with…' (Do I really want to say I'm with my mum?) 'I'm just picking up a few things. What are you up to?'

The tops of her cheeks flushed red slightly, and she giggled nervously. 'It's nothing. I was just going for a walk down by the river.'

Convinced she was meeting someone, I started to back away. 'OK, well I'll see you at school on Monday then.'

She bit her lip and looked around. 'Actually do you want to come with me?'

'OK,' I answered, all too quickly.

We stood at the crossing again, again waiting for that flash, and passed the gallery, the taxi rank and eventually the supermarket carpark. The path that led us down to the river walkway was littered with beer cans, crisp packets and takeaway boxes. Kicking a can aside, I felt a slight twinge of sadness that we had taken something that belonged to nature and besieged it with remnants of our over-indulgent lives.

'Over here,' Izzy called out, gesturing me to the passage under the bridge. Her body faded into the shadows in front of me, but I could hear her voice calling out to me still.

Even though it wasn't low, I ducked my head as I got deeper under the bridge. 'You're not going to kill me and dump my body in the river, are you?'

She jumped out of the shadows back into the sunlight and laughed. 'No, but I am going to make you do something illegal.' She slid the bag off her shoulder until it dropped to the floor. Bending down, she rustled inside it for a couple of minutes before finally pulling out two long silver cans. One had a blue lid to it, and the other had a black lid. They looked like hairspray cans. 'Here,' she said, tossing the blue can to me.

'What's this for?'

She pointed at the wall to her left, and I suddenly understood why I needed the graffiti paint spray. From floor to top, even inside the archways, were doodles, signatures and even words of political meaning. 'You want me to spray-paint something?'

'Anything you want.' She walked over to the wall and pointed to a verse written in blue. 'That was me last month.'

'How often do you do this?'

'Not often. Just when I need to get out of the house. When I want to piss my dad off,' she said, looking at other people's representations.

I walked closer to hers. '*Swallowed. Followed. Heavy about everything but my love. Swallowed. Sorrowed. I'm with everyone and yet not. I'm with everyone and yet not,*' I read aloud. 'What does that mean?'

'It's nothing. It's just lyrics to a song.' She handed me a can. 'Your turn.'

'I don't know what to write.'

'Don't think, just spray,' she laughed nudging me.

'Is that the paint brand's motto?' I quipped, rolling my eyes. 'OK, here goes.' I loosened the lid off the can until I heard a pop of air, then started shaking it. I could hear a hissing noise from inside the can the harder I shook it. I wondered if I shook too hard that it would explode. I could faintly recall a news article about a defunct paint can that had done that. So, I immediately stopped shaking. Standing at the wall, with my finger on the push button, a thousand words and images whizzed in my head, none gripping on for awareness.

I could feel Izzy's body suddenly closer to mine, the floral smell of her hairspray or perfume or something lingered in the air around me. She leaned in even closer, my entire insides on fire and whispered, 'Don't think.'

I could hear the release of air, the slight moistness of the spray, before I realised that I was finished. Beside Izzy's lyrics, I had doodled the first five notes to Bethoven's *Moonlight Sonata*.

'Are those piano notes?' she asked, touching the wet paint with her fingers.

'Yeah. I told you I didn't know what to write,' I shrugged.

'No, these are perfect.' She read each note carefully, as if she could hear the music in her head too. 'Do you miss it?'

'Playing the piano?'

'Yeah, you said before you used to play. I bet you were good,' she smiled.

'I was going to apply to the Royal Academy of Music in London.'

'And you're not any more?'

I shook my head.

'Why not?'

I shrugged. 'A lot's changed. I just don't play any more.'

'That's a shame, Sam. You should play. Maybe you can play for me one day?'

I smiled back. 'I – '

' – You kids better not be graffiting down there!'

We looked up to see a middle-aged police officer walking briskly through the carpark, heading straight for us. Izzy grabbed the can from my hands and pushed it deep inside her bag, along with hers. Grabbing my hand, she pulled me out from under the bridge and along the walkway. The bridge behind us, we ran up the stairs on the other side of the path. Our bodies moving quickly, I could feel the newspaper slip up from inside my jeans hem and fall to the ground. I turned around to see it opened out on the ground, Charlie's face staring up. But she gripped my hand harder and I didn't break away to go back and get it. I stayed running. I stayed with her.

She grabbed her mouth with her spare hand and stifled a laugh, as we dodged shoppers and teenagers with prams and grocery bags. I looked over at her as she ran beside me. Her hair bounced up and down, just a few inches short of her shoulders. I wondered what she'd look like with long hair. Maybe less of the black eyeliner too.

We slowed to a normal pace once we got back to High Street. Her hand had dropped mine by this point, but I still felt her touch, her warmth, in my palm.

By the time we reached the post office, we were

gasping for breath in between laughing. 'That was close!' she panted.

'Do you think he recognised me?'

'No, he has no idea who we are, don't worry. But we should split up, in case he's still looking for us. See you Monday?'

She brushed a piece of hair from her face, the back of her hand lightly tinted with black spray paint. Her green eyes glistened in the sunlight that seemed to be directed right above her, as if the rays followed her.

'See you Monday,' I said. I started to turn around but stopped so I could watch her walk away. Again the rays followed her across the street as she hurried around the corner and disappeared.

I waited for another moment in case she turned back, then snaked through the clusters of Saturday shoppers to the carpark where my mum sat huddled in the driver's seat with both hands on the steering wheel, staring straight ahead. The hate mail lay on the back seat.

Chapter 11

'Breathe' *(Prodigy, Autumn 1996)*

I had a dream about him again last night. But we weren't running this time. Instead, I dreamt that I was falling. The air frantically whipped at my face so hard that when I awoke, my cheeks tingled and throbbed. There was nothing I could do to stop myself falling, nothing I could reach out for and nothing to cushion the impact. But when I hit the ground, again so hard that I felt it through my body even long after wakening, I realised that I wasn't the only one who had fallen. My brother's body lay next to me. Cold and hard, like a rock, it remained still. When I touched him, he didn't move. When I said his name, he disappeared. And when I woke up, he was still gone.

I wrote about that dream in my journal the next day. During our first session back, Dr Albreck had said to document every dream I could remember and every memory I wanted to forget. Now my journal was getting full, and I would need a new one soon. On some pages there weren't even words, just scribbles, doodles. A couple of pages just had Charlie's name, over and over. I hadn't realised before how fun his name was to write. The coil of the 'C', how you can loop the tip of the 'H' if you want and how the dot on the 'I' can be a blank canvas for a tiny heart or star. My name wasn't fun to write. Three letters. One syllable.

I stared at the pages all the time, even when I wasn't writing on them, wondering if and what my drawings and words revealed. What did they say about me? What answers could they give me?

The drawings and words spray-painted on the outside of our house were much easier to decipher. In fact, they weren't even difficult to begin with. Mostly they focused on the word 'Hell' – 'Go to hell', 'Burn in hell', 'Rot in hell'. The graffiti came in an array of colours – purple, red, blue, green. If it hadn't carried such a heavy meaning, the paint might actually have looked pretty. Like a rainbow.

Similar words were written on our newspapers, if the paperboy actually delivered them that morning. At first the words hurt, but after a while they became familiar and even indicative of our future. Maybe we would go to hell. After a while, words weren't enough. Four nights earlier a brick had been thrown through our living room window, smashing the glass into a million small pieces. Tiny fragments of glass were still being found every day. Only last night, Dad cut his finger on one on the sofa reaching for the remote control. Old wooden boards concealed the hole made by the brick. I didn't know if Dad was going to replace the glass, or just leave the planks up there. Perhaps he was expecting another brick in the near future. We would never be able to sell the house now.

If only Charlie could see us. We were nobodies before the shooting. I wandered through the corridors of Pembrook unseen and unheard, only vaguely known by some for playing the piano in the Academy Showcase concert that previous year. Mum worked dayshifts at Above and Beyond Elderly Housing. Dad constructed mediocre furniture pieces in his garage workshop and sold them to generous family-owned shops in the surrounding villages. However the last piece he had sold, a birchwood armoire, was over two years ago. Even when his 'business' was relatively busy, his day was 30 per cent work and 70 per cent drunk. Mum wished he would get a real job, but I think that was just to stop the drinking.

Now we were the most famous family in the country. Everyone knew Charlie's name and even our faces were familiar. The Macmillan name was a curse. Everywhere we walked, the faces of the victims walked with us. We were perpetually haunted. Endlessly followed. And needlessly blamed.

And that wasn't just it. Each day that passed brought new fears, new anxieties. I felt this heavy blanket on me, suffocating me. I couldn't sleep. I couldn't eat. I wandered between irrational fits of anger and idyllic bouts of numbness. I tossed and turned all night, seeing my brother's face loom over me in the darkness. I saw Charlie everywhere – at the top of the stairs, peering out of his bedroom door, sitting at the dining table. I even thought I saw him walk past me in the hallway at school. My head felt clouded, and my fists pounded at my temples as I sought something, anything. One minute, I wanted to feel and the next, I would have done anything not to feel. I wanted it all to go away. I needed it to go away. I felt like I was going crazy.

Even by the next day, sitting on the steps at the gallery, thoughts of my brother riddled me. My coffee sat untouched on the stone beside me, heat no longer penetrating the cold air around it. Enthusiastic voices and bursts of laughter encircled me, tempting me out of the shadows but every time I opened my mouth to join in, a lump formed in my throat.

'Sam?'

I looked up and saw Izzy had slid closer to me, distancing herself from the group. 'You OK?' she asked.

I shrugged and half-nodded, not sure how honest a response I wanted to give. Was I OK? No, I definitely wasn't OK. That was becoming more and more apparent every waking minute of the day.

Izzy leaned against the stone step, propping her elbow on the next one up. 'Did I ever tell you that Carol drags me to her book club on Saturday mornings when she feels that she has to spend time with me to show off to my dad, but doesn't know what else to do with me?'

'A book club?' I said, wishing I didn't have to engage in trivial conversations.

'It's about as exciting as watching an egg boil.'

'It can't be that bad.'

'The last book they discussed was about a bored housewife who decides to become a financial advisor.'

'And?'

'And nothing, that's it. The whole novel.'

'Wow. So what do you usually do?'

'I sit next to Carol and doodle in my notepad drinking tea with honey. We don't say a word to each other, and she calls that our weekly 'quality time'. She boasts to my dad and their golf club friends about how close we are and what a good parent she is. Anyway, I'm telling you this because on Saturday the book club was held at a colleague's house who lives in Ellenstown, right outside Pembrook.'

'You were in Pembrook?' I asked, feeling my cheeks burn slightly at the mention of my town.

'Not exactly. We drove through it to get to Ellenstown, and I...' She fidgeted with the ends of her hair, twirling it between her fingers. 'Um... I think I saw your house.' Her eyes burrowed a hole into mine, searching for a certain response.

'How did you know it was my house? Do you know my address?'

'No, but I knew,' she said, quietly.

'Oh, right,' I said, quickly understanding what she meant. 'Let me guess, the graffiti sprayed across our house gave it away? Yeah, I suppose it's not difficult to figure out that that's my house.'

She didn't say anything, but just looked at me.

'We're... um... really popular with the neighbours,' I laughed, hearing the phoneyness of my laughter ring in the air.

She didn't laugh. 'I didn't know it was like that for you, for your family,' she finally said.

'I don't really talk about it so you wouldn't know.'

'Why is that?'

'I don't know. Maybe I'm bottling up emotions,' I said, shrugging my shoulders as I quoted Dr Albreck. 'Or maybe I don't feel that I have the right to say anything about it. I mean, I wasn't there. I don't know what it was like. I don't know how scared everyone was. I didn't lose anyone to a homicidal teen – my brother *was* the homicidal teen,' I smiled, my voice dripping in distasteful sarcasm. 'I just don't feel like I have a place in any discussions about what happened at Pembrook. But that doesn't stop everyone from blaming me, of course.'

'What do you want to say?'

'About the shooting? I don't know how I feel exactly, but I want to say "sorry" to the families on behalf of my brother. I would want to offer my condolences, which is what I would have done had I been allowed to go to the funerals or say something to the television crews outside our house.'

'You weren't allowed to go to the funerals?'

I shook my head, and gazed down at the laces on my shoes. Inside, my toes squirmed and slithered uncomfortably.

'Go see the families. Tell them how you feel and offer your condolences,' she said, shrugging her shoulders casually as if she was advising me on what music album to buy or what to order at the cafe. This suggestion weighed heavier than any advice given to me since the shooting.

'They would never let me in the front door, let alone hear what I have to say.'

'So, write to them instead then.'

'I can't. What would I say? "I'm sorry my brother killed your son"?'

'Yes, exactly that. You don't have to send them if you change your mind, but maybe just writing a letter to every family is what you need right now – '

' – Izzy, we're leaving now,' Dougie said loudly, standing over us. 'Sam, you coming to the cafe? I'm starving, and need a burger.' He threw his arm around Izzy's shoulder as she got to her feet.

'No, you go ahead. I'm going to get the bus from the square and head home. I have something to do.' I glanced back at Izzy as Dougie steered her down the street like a little dog on a leash. She also looked back at me, smiling gently.

The silent 40-minute bus ride was all I needed to think about what I wanted to say, because when I got home putting pen to paper was easy. The words were simple and straight to the point – not my finest penmanship – but they were honest and expressed how I felt. That I was sorry for any part I had played and that I, more than anything, wanted them to know how deeply sorry I was for what my brother did to their family. But writing them wasn't enough. Getting those words down on paper didn't leave me feeling lighter or more understood, like writing in my journal did. In fact, I felt more restricted, more censored. So, I posted the letters, and hoped that I had made the right decision for my family. I hadn't.

That Saturday morning I awoke from a nightmare of shrinking walls and falling ceilings to hear the quarrelling voices of my parents coming from downstairs. Staggering down one step at a time, I found my dad hunched over the kitchen counter and my mum soaking her tears with a tissue in the corner by the kettle.

'What is it now?' I asked, a yawn escaping from my mouth.

'I'm sorry, Sam. Did we wake you?'

I stared at my dad, immediately detecting the sarcasm and anger in his voice.

'Are you tired?' he continued. 'You must be. Were you up late writing all night again?'

'Stop it, Dan!' said my mum, throwing her arms down by her side.

'Read it.' My dad slid the newspaper over to me, his hand slightly trembling.

Splashed across the front page was my face and the headline, 'Brother's Daring Confession.' Pictures of a letter I had written sat snuggled underneath the bold-font title. One of the families must have taken my letter to the tabloids. I never saw that coming.

'Here, let me read it to you in case you've forgotten. "*My name is Sam Macmillan. You probably don't know me, but you know my brother, Charlie Macmillan. I'm sorry no one in my family has written to you before. And I'm sorry to bother you now, especially when you're grieving, but I wanted to apologise. I'm sorry for what my brother did to your family. I'm sorry you lost someone because of him. I'm sorry you'll never get to see your son graduate from university. And I'm sorry his life ended. If there is anything that I can do to make this better, please let me know because I don't know how to make this right...*" Shall I go on?'

'No need,' I said, clenching my jaw so tight that it ached.

'Is this what you wanted? Did you write that letter to get attention, Sam?' my dad asked.

'No, of course not! I'm not some depressed teen seeking a little spotlight on myself! I'm not Charlie!'

'Sam,' gasped my mum as she started frantically blotting the tears that streamed down her cheeks.

'What I mean, is that I didn't do it for attention.'

'Then why write that letter?' my mum said, walking closer to me.

'I wrote the letters as a way of saying sorry, I guess.'

'Yes, I know – you wrote the word 'Sorry' eight times,' said my dad, holding up the newspaper. 'Wait, what do you mean "letters"? Are there more?'

'Yes, fourteen. I wrote to all the families,' I muttered, biting down on my lip.

'God almighty!' roared my dad.

'Dan – '

' – Shut up, Linda!' Dad turned back to continue addressing me. 'You wrote letters of apology to all the families? Do you know what you've done? I've had fifteen journalists call me this morning asking about a possible interview with you. Fifteen! There's a reason your mother and I haven't spoken out about this publicly. There's a reason we've been lying low these few months. You reaching out, saying "Sorry", has re-opened the media doors. Our faces are everywhere again. Just look at this paper.'

'We're always in the papers. That never went away.'

My dad waved his hand at me, gesturing me away like I was nothing, a child with no opinions, no feelings, no rights. That angered me. I was a part of this family, and in some ways I was taking the full force of this bomb that devastated our community.

'Do you even know how difficult it is for me in school now? People either hate me or are scared of me. That's never going to change. People are always going to look at me that way,' I said, approaching my father.

He turned to face me, his chest heaving in and out. 'Difficult for you? Don't be so selfish. This is hard for all of us.'

'Not for you, apparently. Nothing's changed for you. You're still holed up in that garage. You have no idea what it's like on the outside for us. You never leave the house. You never have to face anyone. Did you even know that there was a petition going around trying to ban handguns?'

'Of course I did,' he said. 'It's crazy.'

'I can't wait to hear this explanation,' I grinned, knowing that my eyes gave away the bitterness beneath. 'Why is it crazy, Dad?'

'I don't have to do this,' he said, turning to walk back to the garage.

'No!' I roared. 'Talk to me! I'm sick of being ignored!'

'Fine. This petition is a waste of time. People actually think regulating weapons will stop teen violence. If teenagers can't get their hands on guns, then they'll bring a knife to school! This petition isn't addressing the real reason. It's the school system that let us down! If they had only – '

' – If it's not the school system, then it's the videogame companies. And if it's not them then it's the censorship boards who've allow the broadcasting of violent television shows before 9pm. Dad, I've heard it all before! You're deluded! You're blaming everyone else except for yourself! You think you're completely innocent in this!'

'I am!'

'You're not! You think if Charlie had a sober father who didn't bully him and everyone else that he would've shot up a school?!'

The words lingered in the air, its heavy presence pressing down on me. My mother's mouth gaped open, her bottom lip shaking wildly. I couldn't believe that I had said it. I hadn't even realised that I had thought it before just now. Did I really blame my father? Or was I trying to hurt him by saying the one thing that I hoped no one had ever thought outside of these walls? I would never have wanted my father blamed for fourteen deaths. So, why had I said that?

'Dad, I didn't mean that – '

' – I'm going out,' he said, getting his coat on. 'Don't wait up for me, Linda.'

The front door slammed loudly, and I heard a media frenzy erupt outside. My dad shouted, 'No comment' and after a few minutes I heard the roar of the car engine and the squeak of the tyres on tarmac as it sped out of the driveway.

My mum took the box of tissues in her hand and slowly walked to the stairs. Her slippers barely made any noise on the steps, but I knew she had reached the top when her bedroom door closed shut.

My head throbbed and pounded as the silence grew thicker around me. I sat down at the kitchen counter, my bare feet dangling over the edge of the stool and gently tore each page of the newspaper in half. Then I went back upstairs and curled under the blankets in my bed and hummed the rhythm of *Moonlight Sonata* to myself until I fell into a restless and nightmare-plagued sleep for the rest of the day. Every time I closed my eyes, I saw Charlie's face. And every time I opened them, I saw a vast emptiness that would never again be filled.

Chapter 12

'Follow You Down/Til I Hear it From You'
(Gin Blossoms, Winter 1996)

The last week of school before Christmas break was a harmonised ensemble of sounds and voices – the frantic pounding of feet on the stairs, the excited squeals of those going abroad for the holiday, the vibration of Christmas music streaming from classroom radios. A classic Paganini piece. I could hear 'Caprice, no. 5' as students walked as if in fast-forward mode. For me, the last week was as dramatic and torturous as a Beethoven arrangement.

For most, Christmas and New Year embodied family togetherness, strengthened friendships and signified new beginnings. For me, it didn't. It would be our first Christmas without Charlie. Our first Christmas as a family nationally recognised for raising the son who'd go on to kill fourteen people in cold blood. Our first Christmas as a family without a purpose, without a hope. And that was too painful to imagine.

While those around me sat by a tree adorned in fairy lights and sparkling baubles, my family would no doubt be infinitely separated by indestructible brick walls in a cold empty house. While families pulled together to roast turkeys and steam Christmas puddings, my family would likely be coming to the heartbreaking realisation that Charlie was in fact the glue that had held us together for so many years. Without him, every day we risked falling off the shelf and smashing into a thousand shards. To walk through my house was to walk on broken glass, a bitter stroll where the past follows you every step of the way and cuts you deep at every turn.

But that wasn't the only thing that was bringing back the anxiety-produced chest pains and dark thoughts. Christmas meant possibly going two whole weeks without seeing Izzy and Dougie, and my new group of friends who I had grown quite close to over the past month. We'd sat together for lunch almost every day – bar a couple of days when the insults from Noel and his friends got so bad that I had to take my lunch to the office and eat it in the waiting room. They were the reason I got up every morning while my mum curled up on her bedroom floor watching a shaky video of

Charlie at Disney World in 1989. It was because of them that I walked the corridors day after day tolerating pencils, erasers and paper planes being thrown at my head. They were the sole reason why the bottle of painkillers I had taken from my mum's dresser back in August remained sealed shut in the top drawer of my bedside cabinet.

For two whole weeks I wouldn't get passed notes in Physics about the ketchup stain on Mr Stevens' tie, I wouldn't get scribbled invitations to Friday Frenzies and I wouldn't get to walk with them to the Art Gallery to sit on the stairs and debate whether the death of Kurt Cobain was a conspiracy or not. Without school, they wouldn't be able to get in touch with me or more importantly, see me every day and be reminded that I was part of their group now and a valued member. Without school they might forget me, or worse, remember why they should forget me.

By the time Friday came around, I had got myself so worked up into a state of distress that I handed in my English essay late, failed my Physics practice exam, and even skipped writing in my journal. I knew what Dr Albreck would say, that I was being dramatic and verging on obsession. I wasn't obsessing. I was being practical. Those six people were my lifejacket in a rough sea of endless storms and squalls. Without them, I would drown.

The final dismissal bell was swathed in screams and cheers as students funnelled out of classrooms and labs. I stayed behind, waiting for Dougie to come out of Intermediate French. When I saw him, the pit in my stomach got a little lighter.

'Hey,' he said, putting an arm around Izzy's shoulders. Clearly she had forgiven him and their on again/off again relationship was back on. Again. No wonder Debbie compared their toxic connection to that of Sid Vicious and Nancy Spungen. I didn't know who they were, but Debbie told me it hadn't ended well for either of them. I hoped a drunken stabbing wasn't in Izzy's future.

'Hey guys. We heading to the gallery today?' I asked, as Debbie and Worm came up from behind me.

'Can't today. My mum will kill me if I don't go home and pack,' said Dougie.

'Where you heading?' The knot in my stomach began to grow again, its heaviness invading my thoughts.

'We go to the Canaries every year for Christmas. My mum doesn't 'do' cold weather,' he said, giving a wave to a pretty brunette walking past him, a wave that was instantly picked up on by Izzy.

'Who's that?'

'Just a girl in my French class,' he said to her. 'So,

I'm out but let's definitely plan for a New Year's Eve celebration at Izzy's.'

'Isabel's? Is she going to play us her Spice Girls album?' said Max as he approached from behind us and playfully bumped into her.

'Shut up, Max!' she laughed, pretending to punch him.

Debbie and Worm slid into the group. 'Hey Sam, you can meet me at my house, since you know how to get there, then we can head over together?' she said.

'Ooh, how romantic!' said Worm, nudging Max.

Debbie rolled her eyes and waved to the group. As she walked away, I looked at Izzy's face and momentarily thought she looked annoyed. Had I done something wrong? Was she jealous?

I was still analysing her expression by the time Christmas morning dragged in. Pulling the covers off my head, a faint sliver of sunshine sneaked in through the crack in my curtain. Groaning, I ducked under the quilt again, breathing in the warmth. Unable to get back to sleep, I threw off the covers and hauled my body out of bed, not quite ready to face the day.

I glanced back at the carpet beside my bedside table – no stocking this year. Dragging my feet down the stairs, one excruciating step at a time, I heard my dad cough in the kitchen. I paused, waiting for him to finish making his coffee, then when I heard the garage door shut behind him I came down.

Putting the kettle on, I leaned against the counter and took a deep breath. Our first Christmas without my brother. This was it. He really was gone. The living room was empty, void of a tree, presents, snowmen ornaments. My mum probably didn't even know that it was Christmas Day.

Pouring myself a strong cup of coffee with two sugars, I plopped down on the sofa with the remote control in my hand. Hand slightly trembling, I turned the TV on. I didn't know what to expect. Every new headline brought me further anxieties, further pain. I couldn't take any more. At first, a snowman cartoon and a *Top of the Pops* holiday special occupied the first two channels. But before I could take a deep breath, BBC1 was airing its morning news report. Determined to turn the channel, I was stopped by my brother's face suddenly appearing on the screen. The petitions had finally reached the Government. Fifty thousand signatures in less than two months. John Major would announce Downing Street's decision on a vote after the New Year. Until then, we'd have to wait. Again, always waiting.

Mum finally came downstairs around 2pm, in her pale-blue dressing gown and worn-through slippers. I heard the kettle snap on and a long drawn-out sigh release from around the corner.

Clutching the remote in my hand, I cleared my throat. 'Merry Christmas, Mum.'

The air stiffened around me as a sharp silence wafted through from the kitchen. Feet shuffling, Mum slowly entered the living room. 'What did you say?' she asked, tiny little lines splintering all over her forehead like cracked wood.

'I said, Merry Christmas,' I repeated. She stared at me, a heavy vacant expression on her face. 'It's Christmas.'

'When?'

Was she drunk? 'Today, Mum. It's Christmas Day today.'

Heavy footsteps broke the awkward silence that followed as the garage door burst open, hitting the wall loudly. Mum and I turned and stared at him, not knowing exactly what we wanted him to say.

'What?' he said.

'Did you know it was Christmas Day?' Mum asked him, leaning her head slightly towards her left shoulder.

He ignored her question and headed towards the front door. Bending down to grab yesterday's newspaper, I heard him swear sharply under his breath. Marching back, he slammed the newspaper down on the granite counter. 'I'm really getting sick of this. It's about time I had a word with the newsagent. It's their paperboy, you know?'

Edging up the sofa, I leaned over and saw the top of the paper. The words, 'Merry Christmas, Basterds!' were scribbled in black permanent marker across the front page. You couldn't even see the article or headline beneath it, but I think it had something to do with Dolly the cloned sheep.

'He spelled "Bastards" wrong,' I said.

'Dan, are you listening? I said it's Christmas Day,' Mum said again.

'Oh … Merry Christmas,' mumbled Dad, going back to his newspaper.

'You could at least put the newspaper down,' snapped Mum.

'I'm not the one who's been hiding in my room all day. It's bleeding 2pm, Linda?!'

'I haven't been the one hiding! You're always in that garage of yours! What do you do all day, anyway? I hear that woodcutter on all the time. What are you making? A boat so you can bugger off?'

Dad picked up the paper and tossed it near the rubbish bin. 'You could have at least bought the boy a present or something,' he said, striding towards the garage door.

'Me? What about you? You're his parent too!'

The sound of the wood smashing against the

doorframe as it closed combined with the wailing of my mother as she fled up the stairs reminded me why I had been so devastated at school breaking for two weeks. No distractions. No clutter to fill my head making it impossible to fit in those dark thoughts. Nothing to ease the pain, and nothing to stop my parents from bringing on more.

Chapter 13

'She's a Star' *(James, Winter 1996/1997)*

New Year's Eve couldn't come fast enough. Christmas Day was a taste of what the week would look like – night-and-day television reports, long-lens cameras trying to see through our curtains to capture our emotional status, an absent mother and a vacant father. The one thing that didn't fill our house during that week was Christmas. There were no tunes of yuletide joy or merry gentlemen, no snapping of a cracker, no bad jokes and endless flow of mulled wine under the mistletoe. In fact, the Macmillan residence was as unjoyous and unfestive as humanly possible. Dad remained in his prison cell made of brick and wood, and Mum remained in hers, made of tears and hysterics. I, on the other hand, counted the days until New Year's Eve which, I will restate, could not come fast enough.

After almost an hour of standing in front of the mirror in an array of outfits, each as uncool as the last one, I finally grabbed the bus to knock on Debbie's door. Tummy filled with fireworks, I couldn't wait to get to Izzy's house. Tonight felt different. More alive. More real. Tonight was going to be the best night of my life, which wasn't hard considering my previous social life.

One swift knock was all it took before the door swung open. 'Oh, hey Sam. Let me get my coat,' muttered Debbie. She emerged in a black blazer with heavily padded shoulder pads, which oddly matched her black fitted dress that looked like a five-year-old's jumper. She had paired that with blue suede boots and a selection of various metal bangles on her wrist.

'Were we supposed to dress up? Is it a costume party?'

She looked at me, ignored the question and gestured towards the wide-open space behind her house that stretched out into a vast darkness. 'Izzy lives right across there.' Her voice always edged on being monotone, as if she was reading from a script on a television show.

'I thought she lived right next to you?'

'She pretends to, but she lives in the nice neighbourhood. Not here.'

Heading into the darkness, the night air consumed us, drawing us in deeper. The air smelled like a warm hearth, cinnamon and expired milk, which may have been Debbie's perfume. Whatever she was wearing, it hit me at the back of my throat and almost caused me to gag.

'So, how was your Christmas?'

Don't ask. 'Um … OK. You?'

'My mum had to work a double shift so I spent Christmas at my gran's watching the *EastEnders* special. Did you see it?'

'No.'

'Grant cheated on Tiffany. Again.'

'Who's Grant?'

'Grant Mitchell? Phil's brother?'

Now I was really confused. 'Are these real people?'

'Of course not, Sam.'

Convinced our conversation was going nowhere, I concentrated on what I would say when I knocked on Izzy's door. Merry Christmas? Happy New Year? I love you? But when we pulled up to the house, I forgot my options. Standing before us was a huge white building with numerous floors and countless windows.

'It looks like a hotel,' I said, glancing at the fountain to the left of the spiralled cobblestone driveway.

'Yeah, her dad's pretty rich. Owns shares in British Airways or something. He works away a lot, so luckily for us we get to enjoy the heated pool,' she smiled, knocking loudly on the front door.

The heavy door swung open and Dougie and Izzy stood holding hands at the entryway like a couple hosting the neighbourhood soiree. Dougie had one hand stuffed nonchalantly into his jeans pocket, while Izzy pulled desperately at her ripped denim skirt so it would appear to be longer than it actually was. Her hair was pulled over to one side and her left ear displayed fresh piercings all the way up. She didn't look comfortable. She didn't look like herself.

I opened my mouth to say Happy New Year but instead the words, 'You have a pool' came out. I immediately snapped my lips closed and felt my cheeks starting to burn. Was I asking her a question or telling her she had a pool in case she hadn't had the opportunity to glance outside at her back garden? What an idiot.

Izzy glanced nervously at Dougie, as he stifled a laugh. 'Yes,' he said, 'there's a pool, Sam. There's also heated flooring in her dad's upstairs bathroom if you want to check that out too.'

'I need a drink,' said Debbie, pushing past us. Dougie followed her, pointing out the artwork on the walls as if he was showing off the house to a prospective buyer. It made me feel slightly uncomfortable knowing that he'd been here so

many times. This was my first time at her house,
and I hoped the first of many times.

Inside, Izzy's place stretched out and spread
backwards like spilled liquid inching towards the
edge of a table. Cream wallpaper, dotted with an
aubergine swirl pattern, covered the walls floor to
ceiling. A large wooden staircase broke through
the mahogany wooden flooring and reached
upwards to the second level of the house. Looping
and weaving in and out of the bannister railing
was a thick green garland adorned with small red
bows and tiny berries. At the bottom of the stairs,
in the right corner, was a tall evergreen Christmas
tree covered in silver tinsel and cream baubles. A
sparkling white star sat shining on the top of the
tree, above some sparkle-covered pinecones. This
was Christmas.

'Wow,' I said to Izzy, looking all around in
amazement.

'Carol has our cleaner secretly decorate every
year and then takes credit for it. But I'm onto her,'
she said, looking wistfully at the tree in the corner.

'My parents completely forgot about Christmas,
and spent the day arguing and drinking cheap beer,'
I shrugged. 'We didn't even have a tree this year.'

'I guess you win,' she laughed. 'Drink?'

'Yes, please.'

She led me into the kitchen where Debbie was

already polishing off her second drink and Max was flipping a martini shaker around. He threw it behind his back and tried to grab it before it hit the floor and the contents oozed out onto the tiles. He looked up and saw Izzy, and simply said, 'Oops' before picking it up and trying the toss again.

'I don't care,' she said, 'Carol can spend tomorrow cleaning this up. They won't be back until then. They're holed up in some fancy hotel for the night. Didn't invite me, of course.'

Before I could say anything, something to offer a sliver of empathy, Dougie came over and threw an arm over her shoulders. 'Doesn't she look good, Sammy?'

Izzy blushed, and tucked a loose strand of hair behind her ear. She playfully smacked him in the stomach. 'Stop embarrassing me!' But then she looked at me and I could tell that she wanted me to answer.

'Yeah, I guess. I sort of liked her hair before,' I muttered, feeling my cheeks get hot too.

'Nah, she looks just like the girl from the concert video now. Beautiful,' he argued, pulling Izzy in for an awkward kiss.

Izzy gently pushed him away and started back towards the sink area, where Max was slicing a lime on the bare counter. 'I'm getting a drink,' she muttered. Was she mad at something I said? Was I supposed to say she looked good when I didn't think so? She looked like a carbon copy of that music video girl, and in my opinion that wasn't something to boast about.

Worm was setting up paper cups across the dining table and filling each with dark ale halfway to the top. He glanced up and saw me, and smiled. 'Hey Sam, fancy spending the last two hours of 1996 playing Beer Pong?'

His question hit me. In a couple of hours the worst year of my life would be over. Gone would be the remnants of 1996 and in its place 1997 would be born, filled with endless possibilities and promises of new beginnings. This could actually be over for me. And at that moment, nothing sounded more amazing then drinking away the last two hours of 1996 with stale ale and plastic ping pong balls.

Pulling off my denim jacket, I eagerly hurried over to the table. 'Definitely.'

Worm threw his arms up in the air and signalled to Max to come join us. Hearing the martini shaker hit the floor again, I turned and saw Max stepping over another pool of liquid. 'I'm in. Who's first?'

'I am,' I said loudly, as my heart started beating faster. 1996 was almost over. 'What do I do?'

'Bounce the ball off the table and when you get one in, you have to drink what's in the cup.'

'What's in the cup?' I asked.

'Yeah.'

'No, really. What's in the cup?'

'Oh,' Worm said, playfully smacking his forehead. 'A little home-made concoction of ale and sherry.'

That sounded disgusting. But I tossed the ball anyway. It hit off the chandelier and dropped loudly into one of the centre cups. Worm and Max high-fived and started chanting, 'Drink, drink, drink – '

' – Sam, you don't have to drink,' said Izzy coming over to the table.

Without looking at her, I said quietly, 'I do.' And picking up the cup, I tossed the contents back until the plastic ball touched my lips. Cool bubbly liquid trickled down my throat, instantly warming my belly. I was right. It was disgusting. I slammed the cup down on the table, and the entire room erupted in cheers. They were cheering for me. For me. And not because I was leaving, but because I was here and they wanted me to stay. Wiping my mouth with my sleeve, I started cheering right back. I was drinking, and I wasn't going to stop drinking until my mind thought about something else other than my brother.

And I didn't. Ninety-five minutes and ten ales later, I staggered upstairs in search of another bathroom. Worm had disappeared into the one downstairs and from the sounds of it, he was throwing up his ales on the bathroom floor. Poor Carol.

But when I reached the top of the stairs, a faint light from the bedroom beside me lit up my hand as it rested on the bannister. Feeling the soft carpet beneath my soles, I walked into the room, curious but also in search of a bed to lie down on. My head felt woozy and the room started spinning.

The first thing I noticed in the room was a picture of a young woman holding a little girl with long brown hair and freckles around her nose inside a cherrywood frame. It sat on the shelf above a desk adorned with trinkets, postcards of faraway places, Steinbeck novels, Roald Dahl hardcovers and half-open make-up containers. When I got closer, I realised the girl in the photo was Izzy but not the Izzy that I knew today. This Izzy looked bare, stripped down from the harsh make-up and piercings, exposed, vulnerable. But she looked happy. She looked free. This was her bedroom. Everything about this room epitomised the girl that I knew – dark but with slivers of light, angry but soft, confident but always searching for validation.

The walls were decorated with music posters, but streaks of pink wallpaper appeared around the edges and in between the posters. I wondered what was underneath the façade – florals, stripes, maybe even polka dots. Who was Izzy truly, deep down inside without all the make-up and costumes? Did *she* even know?

'Hey pervert, you enjoying creeping around a girl's bedroom?'

I jumped, spinning around and letting the framed picture drop to the carpet. The edge hit the soft bristles and landed photo-side down, the glass thankfully still intact. 'No, I was just … just …'

'Sam, I'm kidding, relax,' she laughed, slowly walking towards me. My breath hitched as she got closer, and I felt my cheeks start to burn slightly. She stopped right in front of me, her long eyelashes curled outwards towards her brow bone. Her face too made-up, she smiled at me, her glossy iridescent pink lips turning up.

I shivered, even though I wasn't cold, and felt the hairs on my arms prickling and standing upright. She leaned in, then bent down to pick up the frame. She skimmed closely past me and sat down on the bed, still holding the frame in her hand.

I shuffled over, and plopped down beside her. The water mattress swayed and wobbled beneath me, like jelly. I grabbed onto the desk edge to steady myself, and to stop myself from vomiting all over her, and heard her laugh quietly beside me.

'So Sam, are you having fun tonight?'

'Yeah, definitely. You?'

'It's OK,' she said, gazing down at her fingers as they interlaced in her lap.

'Is everything OK? Where's Dougie?'

'I have no idea,' she shrugged.

'What are your New Year's resolutions for 1997?' I asked, nudging into her.

She nudged me back. 'To not be so afraid.'

'What are you afraid about?'

'Nothing. Everything. I don't know,' she said, running her hand through her hair.

'Are you applying to university?'

'You're really asking me about my educational plans for after the summer right now?' she laughed. 'No, I don't think so. Although my dad would argue otherwise.'

'What would you do instead?' The sounds slurred out of my mouth sloppily.

'Maybe travel.'

'Are you going to visit all of those places on your desk?'

'You saw the postcards on my desk?'

'Yeah, well I wasn't rifling through your things. I just saw them there – '

' – I want to visit all those places – California, Australia, Thailand, Bali. I want to go everywhere. Anywhere but here,' she said, tapping the photo frame against her thigh gently.

'When was the photo taken?' I asked, gesturing to the frame in her hands.

'Just before my mum died,' she said, touching the glass gently with her fingers.

'Oh. That's your mum?'

She nodded slowly, as if she was digesting the words. 'She died when I was thirteen. She had cancer, so it wasn't like it was a surprise or anything. But to me, it was.' She bit down on her lip but I could see it trembling underneath her teeth. 'No one expects someone to die. It's always a surprise, you know? Oh I'm so stupid, of course you know. Sorry, Sam.' She shook her head and ran her fingers through her newly cropped hair. Up close I could see the redness around the piercings on her ears. They looked painful, constricting.

'Don't apologise. This is about you. I'm sick of conversations about me,' I slurred, my hand itching to touch her face. 'Your mum, she's beautiful.'

She nodded and smiled. 'Yeah, she really was.'

'Like you,' I said, the words slipping out with an ease that could only be credited to the ale.

'Yeah, right. You're just drunk. Ugh, my hair is ridiculous here,' she scoffed.

'Actually, I quite like it,' I shrugged.

'Really?'

'Yeah, you look … real.'

'I don't look real now?'

'No, it's not that. You just look like yourself in that photo – you look happy.'

'What is it about you, Sam?' she smiled, leaning into me.

'What do you mean?'

'You're so much cooler and wiser than you give yourself credit for. You should stop being so hard on yourself. I have a New Year's resolution for you – Be more in the moment. Let go.'

Let go.

Below us voices grew louder, chanting down from ten as the seconds closed in on midnight. Ten. Nine. Eight. 'Izzy?' Six. Five. Four.

'Yeah?'

Two. One. I quickly leaned in and pressed my lips against hers. She didn't push me away, in fact she placed her hands on my shoulders and returned my kiss. I raised my hand up, and slowly touched her cheek, pulling her in more. Our lips parted, and we slowly moved away from each other.

'What was that for?' she asked, her eyes wide and alert.

'I was trying to be more in the moment,' I shrugged sheepishly.

She softened, her pursed lips breaking into a gentle smile. 'Happy New Year, Sam.'

'What the hell is going on here?'

We both leapt off the bed, and spun around. Standing in the doorway was Dougie, his body slightly swaying and hitting against the wooden frame. 'You're unbelievable, Sam. I take pity on you, invite you to hang out with my friends, take you under my wing, protect you, and this is how you repay me? By sneaking around with my girlfriend?'

'No, you have to understand. I wasn't kissing Izzy … well, I was, but it wasn't intentional. It was just a spur of the moment thing,' I blurted out, rushing towards him.

He moved past the doorway, deeper into the room. 'Spur of the moment, huh?'

'Yes!' I exclaimed.

'Like this?'

Before I could ask him what he meant, I felt his fist come into contact with my jaw. I heard a popping sound and felt a sharp pain spreading through my lower face. I collapsed to the carpet, my eyes hazy.

'Dougie!' I heard Izzy scream.

'You want her? She's all yours,' he hissed at me, staggering back out of the room.

The last image I saw, before I threw up all over her carpet, was Dougie walking away and Izzy running after him.

Chapter 14

'Alone' *(Dinosaur Jr., Spring 1997)*

I awoke the next day fully dressed on top of my bed with a splitting headache and an even worse pain in my jaw. Touching my face, the skin burned under my fingers and I could only imagine the gigantic bruise that was flourishing there. The pain only brought back memories of the night before, and a deep ache settled into the pit of my stomach. I had kissed Izzy. Dougie had punched me. Now I was remembering. I wondered how long I should wait before calling Dougie to say sorry and beg for his forgiveness. Deciding on one day – to allow egos to unbruise – I dragged myself out of bed, brushed my teeth six times and stumbled down the stairs hoping Mum had remembered that it was New Year's Day.

It turned out, she had. And she had started cooking a lunch. So, while Dad sat on the sofa with a six-pack and the remote control, avoiding the news channels, Mum began frantically chopping and slicing in the kitchen. Around 3pm, the smell of roast beef and baked root vegetables wafted up the stairs and under my bedroom door.

'Sam? Lunch is ready.'

Pausing my videogame, I took a long inhale and enjoyed the memories that came with that Sunday lunch smell – family meals, lazy afternoons in front of the TV, and the occasional boardgame. I swung my legs off the bed and threw down my controller. It landed upside down on the blue carpet, displaying the initials CM painted on with Mum's red nail varnish. My console had once been Charlie's. He had got it two years earlier when it officially came on the shelves. It was big news everywhere. A Sony PlayStation.

People immediately blamed inappropriate videogames for the school shootings. Videogames came right before the finger pointing was directed towards rock music, before moving on to bad parenting, bullying, too much sugar, a lack of discipline, depression and, finally, drugs. The funny thing was that Charlie never played videogames much at home. Shortly after he had got it as a birthday present, he got bored with it, instead wanting to focus more on his drawings. He knew how much I loved to play, so he eventually moved it into my room. He played at Adam's, but only because they lacked much else in common. Charlie didn't share many common interests with people his own age. Any age, actually.

Shambling down the stairs, I heard Dad's slurred speech as he entered the dining room. 'How many times do we have to do this? What is it going to take for you to understand that there are only three of us. Yet – again – here I see four placemats, four plates and four glasses. Four. Four!'

I felt the wall tremble followed by the sound of smashing glass and broken china.

'Dan, stop!' my mum wailed, as her voice cracked. Her angry cries soon turned into deep sobbing as I heard her body drop to the floor.

Rushing down the stairs, I charged into the dining room and found not just Mum on her knees crying but Dad too. Shards of glass and thick slabs of china littered the dining room floor. I inched backwards, their collective sobs filling the room quickly, suffocating me. Their tears were drowning me, drowning us. Our family was falling apart and there was nothing – not even happy memories of Charlie – that could mend the irreversible distance between us. Like the dinnerware that lay around my feet, we were broken.

Rushing upstairs, I pushed open my brother's bedroom door and felt the cold air of emptiness hit me like a brick wall. Gently closing the door behind me, I took a deep breath trying to smell my brother's presence. All around me I saw it – his clothes on the floor, his sketches on the easel – but I couldn't feel it. Would I ever feel it again?

Searching for a piece of him, a fragment of the warm spirit that I remembered, I began opening the drawers of his bedside cabinet. The top drawer held a sketchbook and some gradient pencils. The second drawer housed some odd socks and a copy of *The Catcher in the Rye*. But it was the bottom drawer that reached in and pulled the breath from my lungs. Nestled between Mendal W. Johnson's *Let's Go Play at the Adams'* and Dad's childhood copy of *Lord of the Flies* was a photo of Charlie and me at Harper's Beach when we were young.

I was six years old when it was taken, and I knew that because that was how old I was when I lost my first tooth, which unfortunately was a front tooth. I remembered that day clearly. I remembered the blood on my fingertips, the tooth in the palm of my hand, the warm saltiness of the blood on my lips. I had cried, even though Charlie had told me that losing my baby teeth was a sign that I was getting older, growing up. Those were words that I wanted to hear at the time, but now that reassurance would have terrified me. If this was my first taste of what growing up was all about, then I didn't want it. I wanted to stay young forever. I wanted to remain innocent, ignorant of what went on outside my window. I wasn't ready. Not now. Please, not now.

The edges of the photo curled inwards and there was a slight crease down the middle, but it was undeniable – we were happy. Charlie had his arm around me and I was grinning to the camera, Mum having rewarded me for being so brave with a trip to the beach that afternoon. Our hair was wet having just come in from the ocean, and our noses and cheeks were streaked with a gentle sunburn. I looked around Charlie's room, at the paint streaks on the wall, the hurried smudgings of black chalk on the easel. Like the frame in Izzy's room, this photo also didn't fit here. Or did it? Every day was a war in my head about the boy I knew and the boy I thought I knew. And that night, as I huddled under the covers in my brother's bedroom, I began slipping into the vast darkness that was swallowing my family. Its dark walls and shadowed ceilings comforted me in a way that reality never would. It didn't care that I wasn't coping, it didn't care that I missed my brother, in spite of what he did. Darkness was all I had. It was safe there, predictable. And as my eyelids got heavier, I pulled the photo in closer to my chest and closed my eyes, hoping that I'd never wake up.

But I did. Around midnight, a thick chill washed over my body and I woke up shivering. The light from the moon left white stripes across Charlie's walls and bed covers. I pulled the quilt up further, until the fabric touched my neck and sat up. Nestled in the corner of the bed, I wrapped my arms around my legs and tried to make myself as small as possible. The photo lay only inches from my feet, but I didn't reach out to grab it. I let it lie there, glistening under the harsh glow from the streetlamps. As I rocked gently back and forth, Dougie's face from New Year's Eve burned into my mind. He was so angry at me. Was he still? I had to find out. I had lost everything. I couldn't lose my friends too. Not now.

Still shivering, I placed my feet on the cold floor and zigzagged my way through the clothes on the floor out of Charlie's room. A faint light slipped out from under my mum's bedroom door and I knew she was awake. I guess none of us were sleeping much these days.

Carefully picking up the telephone, I unwound the cord and carried it back to my room. I closed the door, tucking the cord underneath, and sat on my bedroom floor. Leaning against the door, I dialled Dougie's number, having memorised it. It rang out for a long time and just when I was about to hang up, someone answered.

'Hello?' It was a woman. And she sounded confused.

'Hi. Is Dougie home?'

'It's almost 1am, I should hope he's home.' Now she sounded angry.

'Can I talk to him?'

I heard a tapping, like the receiver being placed on a hard surface, and footsteps. 'Douglas? There's someone on the phone for you ...' More footsteps. 'Do you know what time it is?'

'I know, Mum ... hello?'

Now that he was on the phone, I didn't know what to say, or where to start.

'Hello? Is anyone there?'

'Yeah, it's me,' I finally said.

'Who's me?'

'It's Sam.'

'Sam? It's almost one in the morning.'

'I guess I didn't realise how late it was ... were you sleeping?'

'What do you want, Sam?'

Straight to the point. Like me, Dougie wasn't much for trivial small talk.

'I want to explain what happened on New Year's Eve – '

' – I know what happened. I was there, remember?'

'Yes, but it wasn't what you think it was.'

'Oh, so you weren't kissing my girlfriend?'

'Well... yes, I was but – '

' – So it's exactly what I thought it was.'

'It's not like you haven't cheated on Izzy before.' I instantly regretted the words and wished I could suck them back in again. But I couldn't. And they were heard.

'Look, Sam, I've been thinking and I don't think it's such a good idea for you to hang out with us any more – '

' – No, wait – '

' – There's a lot of media attention on you and your family right now, and I don't want me and my friends getting pulled into it – '

' – Wait, Dougie. I – '

' – I've gotta go. My mum is working early shift tomorrow,' he said, his voice flat and void of expression.

And it was done. 'OK.' It was all I could muster.

'See you around.'

'See you around,' I repeated. Before I could say anything else – something to change his mind, to prove to him that I wasn't my brother, that I could make up for my mistakes – he hung up. And all I was left with was the dialling tone and my shallow breaths. What had I done?

Chapter 15

'One Headlight' *(Wallflowers, Spring 1997)*

The morning before school started back, I stood in front of the mirror longer than usual. I had gone back to wearing the same clothes that I had worn before I met Dougie and Izzy, but the reflection before me wasn't the same person as before. I barely recognised myself. Most teenagers, and adults, returned after Christmas indicative of a two-week break. They're rested, rejuvenated, and even carrying a little extra weight from the mince pies and tins of Quality Street. But me, I looked worse than ever. The boy staring back at me looked aged, tired, defeated. I had black circles under my eyes, my hair was grown out and dishevelled, and the clothes that once fitted me hung from my bony frame. I had hit rock bottom, and I hoped that I didn't have further to fall.

I hadn't heard from anyone in Dougie's circle since New Year's Eve. My evenings had gone back to solitary periods in my bedroom staring at the pages of a book I wasn't even reading. And when I considered getting back to the piano, I reminded myself why it sat with a thick layer of dust on the top. I wasn't the same. Things just wouldn't go back to normal just because I wanted it so. And it was pointless to try otherwise. The only thing that comforted me in the smallest possible way, was believing that it couldn't get much worse.

But the moment my feet touched down on the concrete off the bus, I knew that the hole that had swallowed me was much deeper than I had thought. Folding tables were scattered around near the steps to the school's main entrance. The tables were littered with pale-blue flyers and the grass around was blanketed with hundreds of feet – students, parents, neighbours – people I didn't recognise but who seemed to know me as soon as I walked through the school gates.

The air around them grew silent and whispers broke out, causing crashing waves of suppressed sounds. Everyone was looking at me, and I didn't need an explanation. I knew why. I would always know why.

I saw Max leaning against the stone pillar by the school steps watching the crowds gather, and hurried over to him. He saw me and tried to pretend not to. When he began walking away, I called out his name so loud that he couldn't ignore me. 'Max!'

He froze, turned around and painted a fake expression of casualness on his face. 'Oh hey, Sam. Didn't see you there.'

Liar.

'What's going on?'

'Sorry, Sam. I don't want to get in the middle of this, I've known Dougie much longer than I've known you – '

' – No, not that. Dougie's made that perfectly clear. I mean, what's going on here?' I said, pointing to the tables set up.

'Oh, that. It's all over the town.'

'What is?'

'There are tables set up outside the library and the shops on High Street too. They're even going door to door in some towns. Last night, my mum – '

I left Max still talking, not even sure if he'd noticed that I'd gone, and pushed through the crowds, feeling eyes burning into the back of my head as I weaved in and out. Finally the last few bodies parted, and I found myself standing at one of the tables. White papers filled with scribbled signatures tucked neatly into metal clipboards. Beside those lay dozens of the blue flyers, a familiar face posted on each one. My brother's face. Under a black-and-white image of his yearbook photo from last year read the words, 'Stricter gun laws so there will never be another Charles Macmillan in our schools.'

I winced, not at the particular image they choose – the one where he stared directly at the camera with empty cold eyes – but because they used his full name. He hated 'Charles'. No one ever called him that. But 'Charlie' was too friendly, too approachable for a witch-hunt.

'Sign our pledge to vote on the 16th of April,' urged a table bystander, as he handed a ballpoint pen to me.

All around people stopped whispering and watched to see if I would take it. They stared at me with the same curious expression that I would expect to see on a child's face at the zoo. Was this all a show for them? Did they expect me to entertain them?

Not one to disappoint the masses, I grabbed the pen and scribbled my name under the cafeteria lady's. More whispers broke out, this time with more urgency. I turned around and raised the pen up high so spectators at the back could see too. There it was, everyone – my name, Sam Macmillan. Barely of voting age, and I had pledged my support for the banning of all handguns in the country. They were right. There would never be another Charles Macmillan.

My hand slightly trembling, I dropped the pen on the table, took a blue flyer and walked away. Pushing my way through the crowds, I walked into the school and proceeded to have one of the worst days since it had happened. Kids I didn't know pointed at me in the corridors, Noel persuaded everyone to refuse to sit near me in English, and teachers acted jittery around me as if I also was harbouring secret thoughts deep down about death and murder. But that wasn't the worst part. For the first time since I had arrived, Dougie ignored me. He sat at the table furthest away at lunch with everyone, and the spot on the bench where I usually sat was filled with his rucksack. The message was clear – 'You're not welcome.'

And while I sat staring into a cold bowl of pasta and shredded cheese, Izzy gave me a sympathetic and apologetic smile from across the cafeteria as she sat loyally next to Dougie. I didn't know what I had expected from her. I was smart enough to know that the kiss didn't mean as much to her as it did to me. But I wasn't smart enough to realise that by Monday morning she'd be right back with Dougie playing the whole 'I was just drunk' card.

By the time the bell rang at 3.10pm, I had unanswered two passed 'I'm sorry' notes from Izzy in Maths, failed to avoid a rubber being thrown at my head in Physics, and had a wave rejected by

Worm. Not even Worm was talking to me. I had done it. I had managed to lose all my friends in one night. I had nobody. I was lonely, miserable, lost. And as the weeks went on, it seemed like that was what everyone wanted. No one wanted to see me happy, doing well at school, moving on. That would have been too easy for my family. We had to show we were in misery. People wanted to see us buried under the immense guilt and pain that we should have been feeling. And even then they wouldn't be satisfied. We would never be excused from this nightmare. We would forever serve Charlie's sentence.

Jaw clenched so tight that it ached, I snatched up my bag and pushed back my chair. Marching through the door, I hurried down the hall, the walls suddenly seeming too narrow, too stifling. I needed to get out. My head was going to explode. Is this what Charlie felt?

'Sam!'

I turned around to see Izzy rushing towards me. She glanced over her shoulder briefly, as she stopped near me. 'Did you get my notes in Mr Fitzgerald's class?'

'Yeah, I did.'

'You didn't write back?'

'I didn't want to talk to you over notes,' I shrugged.

'Oh. How have you been?'

'Are you and Dougie back together?' I didn't have time for small talk. I needed answers. I had enough uncertainty going on right now.

'Well ... we talked the next day. You see, I had way too much to drink – '

' – You know what, Izzy? I'm done.'

'What does that mean?' she asked, her eyes narrowing.

'It means that I don't care what you do any more. If you're not happy, then break up with him. If you're happy then stay with him. Do whatever you want, just leave me out of it. I have enough shit going on right now.'

She leaned away from me slightly, cheeks red and mouth slightly agape. For a second I thought I was going to make her cry, which would have just topped my day. 'I'm sorry, Sam,' she stuttered. 'You're putting me a difficult position.'

'Am I? Because unless I'm crazy like my brother, I thought you wanted to kiss me. I've been feeling for weeks that you're into me. Did I imagine all that? Have you just been leading me on for fun?'

'No! Well ... I ... I don't know what to say.'

'If you don't know what to say to me then you mustn't have anything to say,' I said, turning around to leave.

'Sam.' She grabbed me by the arm. 'Can we still be friends?'

'I don't see how that's possible. Dougie hates me and no one else is talking to me, which I guess is what I deserve. You better go before he sees us talking,' I said, gently sliding out of her grasp. I glanced behind to see if she was still watching me, but she was already gone.

When I reached outside, most of the tables had been cleared but blue flyers still littered the grass. Every step I took, my brother's eyes stared up at me. His face haunted me, the blue paper sticking periodically to the soles of my shoes. I couldn't avoid stepping on him, his image was everywhere. His mistakes were everywhere.

Heat tingled and spread up my neck to my face, like a growing fire. I couldn't take this much longer. My jaw quivered, like I was going to cry and I wiped a hand across my face as I left the school grounds. I didn't want people to see me cry, to see me beaten.

I avoided the main streets, not wanting to face more blue flyers, and took the bus back to Pembrook. But instead of going straight to the Family Counselling Clinic, I took a detour through the cemetery. I figured I could visit Charlie's 'grave' on my way to my appointment with Dr Albreck. I needed to be alone right now, and I couldn't think of anywhere more deserted than my brother's empty gravestone.

But it wasn't deserted. When I got to the cemetery, I could see a group of teenagers huddled together. A couple of kids were laughing while some were bent over, their faces out of view. I thought they were just messing around, drinking beer, passing time in one of the few places they knew where there would be no police. But when I got closer, I realised they were huddled around a gravestone. My brother's gravestone. And as my feet came to a painfully slow speed, I finally understood why they were there. They weren't hanging out, or drinking beer. They were spraying 'Murderer' across Charlie's stone in thick dark-red spray paint.

'Hey!' I pounded the ground towards them, divots of mud springing up around my feet as I got faster. 'Hey! Get away from there!'

They scattered, throwing the paint can into the trees beside them, and ran through the cemetery laughing. I chased after them, tiring quickly. Marching back to Charlie's plot, I sank to my knees. My shadow loomed over the stone marker, the red paint trickling in different directions and stretching out the letters into streams of blood. It was ruined. The last piece of his remembrance was ruined. Every rose my mum left at his grave was taken, every photo she placed on top of the stone was ripped in half, every bulb she planted was pulled out by its roots. And now, the stone itself was destroyed. We couldn't afford to replace the marker, so unless Mum could scrub it off with her buckets of warm soapy water, the word 'Murderer' would forever shroud Charlie's stone, and my last memory of him.

My body felt warm, the heat building within me. When would this stop? When would we be allowed to grieve for my brother, and move on? I clambered to my feet, the grave no longer meaning anything to me. Snatching up my bag, I stormed past the remaining graves, all capturing kind messages for loved ones, and headed to my four o' clock appointment.

When I got there, Dr Albreck was running late. Instead of waiting patiently in the seating area, I stood near the receptionist's desk. Drumming my foot off the thin metal ventilation panel beneath me on the skirting boards, the noise vibrated through the waiting room. The receptionist stared at me, but I didn't stop. I couldn't stop. The movements weren't mine any more. I couldn't control them.

By the time she finally saw me, my impatience and anger had spread all over my body and I couldn't even sit down in my usual armchair. I leaned my body against her filing cabinets and bounced off them, feeling them shift and slide away under my weight. When they reached the wall the edges banged softly against the paint, speeding up as my movements got faster, harder. I didn't turn around, but knew if I did that I would see black marks on the wall from the cabinets.

'Sam, what's wrong?' Dr Albreck asked, in that dull emotionless tone that she often used with me, as if she was chastising me like a small infant. I should have stuck with the counsellor that wanted to be my 'friend'.

'Nothing. Why would anything be wrong?' I shrugged.

'Your body is telling me that it's angry, maybe even frustrated.'

'Is my body also telling you that it's bored, maybe even done with this?'

'Done with what? What are you done with, Sam?'

'You. This. Talking about my feelings, moving to a new school, trying to make friends, pretending as if no one remembers that my brother killed half his school. What's the point? Where's it got me? People at school think I'm a freak, my parents can't stand to be in the same room as each other, they don't even acknowledge my existence, and my brother's still dead. Nothing I do – nothing you say – can make this better for me!'

I kicked off the cabinet and felt my hand shoot

across the desk. Books hit the floor beneath Dr Albreck's shoes, and pens trickled off the desk. Papers floated in the air and softly landed like torn feathers from a bird. My chest heaved in and out as I looked down at the mess in front of me. Tears welled up in my eyes and threatened to spill over. I roughly rubbed my sleeve over my eyes, and felt warm tears seep into the fabric. I was crying. I was finally crying. But once it started, it wouldn't stop.

Dr Albreck rose slowly to her feet, and approached me cautiously. 'Sam, I know you're hurting – '

' – No, you don't. You have no idea what I'm feeling. No one does. But everyone tries to guess.'

She reached out and gingerly rested a hand on my shoulder. Her touch burned into me like scorching embers, so I shifted away from her. Her hand dropped down back to her side, and she gave me a sympathetic head tilt. 'This will get better. I promise.'

'I don't see how. I really don't. Nothing will bring him back. He's still gone, and do you know what the worst part is? No one will ever know my brother like I did. No one will ever know how funny he was. No one will see his paintings, if they even knew that he liked to paint. Nobody knows him … I mean, *knew* him.'

'Sam, your brother will always be remembered
– '

' – Yeah, as a murderer. That's all he'll ever be.
So maybe I should remember him like that too.
Maybe it'll hurt less.' I stood up, swinging my
backpack over my shoulder, and walked out. The
door slammed shut behind me, sealing in empty
promises and meaningless words.

I went home, but instead of going in and facing
the sullen expressions of my fragile selfish parents,
I slid open the garage door and got my bike. Thick
cobwebs already wound around the spokes and
handle bars, but I didn't bother to pull them off.
I didn't care. All I wanted to do was bike over to
the west end of town and knock on Adam's door.
I wanted to see the face of my brother's supposed
best friend. I wanted to hear his excuses.

Pulling up outside, I glanced around and
immediately felt the remnants of the summers
spent picking Charlie up from this exact spot, even
though it was January. Feeling the absent sun on
the back of my neck, I remembered getting out to
let my brother ride in the front and to pet Adam's
dog. The big brown Labrador would run to the
car to greet us and push his wet muzzle into me
when I climbed out. I would kneel on the grass and
tickle his belly when he rolled over. We must have
stopped here about a dozen times last summer.

Hours of videogames helped alleviate the minutes spent interacting with Dad every day. They never saw eye to eye. Now they never would.

'What do you want?'

I glanced up and saw Adam leaning out of the upstairs window. His hair was hidden under a black cap and I could see the dark circles around his vacant eyes from down below.

'I'm Sam, Charlie's brother,' I called up.

'Jesus, Sam. I know who you are! What do you want?'

'To talk, I guess.' I don't know why I had imagined this going differently. Adam hadn't seen me since it happened and I was probably the last person he wanted to see standing on his front garden.

'I can't talk to you.'

'Why not?'

'I'm not allowed to. My mum will kill me for even opening the window,' he said, looking up and down the street.

'Well, is she here now?' I asked, shrugging my shoulders.

'No... but – '

'– Adam, I promise if you come down and talk to me, I won't bother you again. I just need five minutes.'

The window slammed shut, the curtain falling

heavily back in place. I turned around and began walking back to the road with my bike. A familiar sound of creaking and popping wood made me turn around. Adam stood in the doorway, his body leaning against the frame. 'I can't let you in,' he said, shaking his head.

'It's OK, I don't need to come in.' I laid my bike down and hurried up to the door, but when I got there the words got stuck in my throat. He wouldn't look me in the eye. And although his posture tried to come across as strong and somewhat nonchalant about the past few months, his hands trembled and beads of sweat formed quickly along his hairline.

'You have four minutes left,' he said, finally meeting my gaze.

'Right ... I just wanted ... needed to know what happened.'

He raised his eyebrows and stared at me as if he didn't recognise me. 'You know what happened. Why do you want to rehash this?'

'Have you seen the voting tables all over town? They're everywhere, even outside my new school. I'm not the one rehashing things. Besides, I know the facts, but what I don't know is why. You hung out with Charlie, you knew him. He must have told you something. Did you notice anything? Did he seem depressed to you? Mentally unstable?'

'Sam, those are a lot of questions to answer in three minutes,' he gasped, raising his hand up to his face. 'I didn't know Charlie. Nobody knew Charlie. We didn't really hang out, not in the sense where we talked or anything. He came over, we played videogames, and he went home. That was pretty much it. Besides I hadn't seen him since the Christmas before. We had a fight and never hung out again.'

'What did you fight about?'

'It was stupid. He took it too far.'

'Can you tell me?'

'He usually sat by himself at lunch, that's what he preferred or that's what he said anyway, and one day some guys from the rugby team started giving him a hard time calling him weird and a loner. And he got mad that I didn't do anything, like I could have.'

'What did you do?'

'I pretended I didn't know him. I maybe even laughed a little too. Yes, I know that was probably wrong or whatever but what was I supposed to do? Those guys didn't leave you alone once you were on their radar. They were on you every day – tripping you in the corridors, sticking notes to your back, locking you in the bathroom, hiding your bag. It only stopped when they moved on to someone else. I wasn't going to be that someone else. Anyway, your brother was pissed off and stopped coming round after that. I never saw him again, except for in the corridors and he just ignored me.'

'Rightfully so. I can't believe you didn't stick up for him. You were his only friend,' I said, shaking my head. I turned and began walking away, hearing Adam's frantic steps behind me. I spun back around. 'Why didn't you call? Send a note? Flowers? What kind of a friend are you? You didn't even come to his funeral!'

'I thought he was cremated?'

'See, you don't even know that!' I laughed. 'And for your information, he was cremated! Which is still a funeral. If you care.'

'Hey, you have no idea what I'm going through! Don't come over here and make me feel bad. I didn't do anything wrong! And everyone looks at me as if I was in on it, as if I was collaborating with Charlie and feeding him names. 'Here, Charlie, here's one for the list – kill Stephen McCain because I don't like the way he looked at me in Physics today!' You know what? I did myself a favour that day by not sticking up for him! I'm glad we weren't friends at the time! I just wish everyone else knew that too!'

'Adam?' We both turned and saw his neighbour standing outside – with one hand on her door in case she needed to shut herself inside for safety. 'Adam, do you want me to call the police?' she said, looking at me with fear visible in her wide prying eyes.

'No, Mrs Bremner. Sam is just leaving,' he called back.

She nodded once, glanced back at me then slammed her door shut. I could see her face still watching us, partially hidden by her net curtain.

'Great, now she's going to call my mum. Thanks a lot. Look Sam, I can't help you. I don't know what Charlie was thinking. Maybe the papers are right, maybe he was on drugs, or depressed or something. How else could a person do something like that?'

Chapter 16

'Sunday Morning' *(No Doubt, Spring 1997)*

By the time the weekend finally dragged in, I was still plagued by Adam's last words before he closed the door in my face. 'How else could a person do something like that?' When I awoke that morning, I awoke with a single objective in my mind. Skipping breakfast, and the awkwardness of entering the kitchen amidst yet another screaming match between my mother and father, I walked to my usual bus stop. But instead of a ticket to Knightsbridge, I bought a return to the city train station. And when I got there, I boarded the 8.47am train to the one place no one expected me to go to – Robert Hurd's hometown.

I rested my head against the glass and stared at the trees and farmland that blended together into one green paint streak, much like Charlie's artwork. Scattered among the farmhouses, hills and occasional sheep, were isolated pockets of small communities, villages much like Pembrook. But they didn't carry the same weight of grief. They hadn't faced loss like we had. They were safe in their brick homes, offices, single-floor buildings and brown-roofed schools. Or were they?

If my parents had found out what I was doing, where I was going, I would be grounded for weeks, maybe even the rest of the school year. Eyes were on us at all times, they told me, but yet as the train moved effortlessly and dream-like through the vast countryside, I didn't feel eyes on me. For the first time in seven months I felt invisible, free of judgement.

Five peaceful hours later, I awoke from a restful nap to a place that was quiet, vacant and tainted as much as Pembrook. I was here. Sliding out of my seat, I disembarked at a station where no one else followed me. Curious eyes peeked through the windows out to the empty streets, as the train continued on to London Paddington.

Within moments, a light misty rain settled on the sleeves of my raincoat. Slipping the hood over my head, my feet pounded the exit stairwell until I reached the bypass. Even though a seven-foot man could easily walk through the tunnel, I ducked feeling the ceilings and walls begin to close in.

Out in the open again, I traced my path to the town centre using a stained map on the back end of a billboard. Red marker crossed out the locations where people had fallen during Hurd's shooting spree. Retracing his steps and getting the answers I needed wouldn't be difficult, it seemed.

My first stop was the local library where I would begin my research. Pushing open the door, a whispered conversation ceased immediately when I entered. Assuming they recognised me, my head dropped. But when they recommenced their local gossip session, I took a deep sigh of relief. Here, even I went unnoticed.

'Can I help you?'

I turned to find a grey-haired woman behind the sign-out desk, flicking a ballpoint pen between her fingers.

'Yes, I need to do research for a school essay but I don't have a membership card.'

'Do you want to sign up for one today? Do you have a bill or bank statement from your parents proving residency in this town?'

'No, I don't. My parents left early this morning before I could ask them, but I really need to finish this essay today.'

'Well ... I can sign you in temporarily for today but I can't let you sign any books out until you speak to your parents,' she shrugged, dragging over the sign-in book. 'Name?'

'Um ... Douglas Morris.' I stole a kiss from his girl, and now I was stealing his identity.

'OK, Douglas, I just need you to sign right here.'

Even down to how I grasped the pen, I imitated how Dougie would sign his name, probably an over-inflated D, followed by a personalised touch at the end. Giving it way too much thought, I finally settled on an underscored line through the 'e'. I immediately regretted my choice.

'Non-fiction is in aisles 4–8, teen fiction is downstairs and historical studies is on this floor by the bathrooms.'

'What if I wanted to research an article in the local newspaper that was printed years ago?'

'Then you'd go to archives, which is downstairs. First set of glass doors on your right.'

'Archives' was the room that I spent the next two hours in. I looked through every newspaper from the day of the shootings until the enactment of the 1988 Firearms (Amendment) Act, similar to what people were trying to accomplish in Pembrook now. At first, articles blended into each other, the content being very much the same, if not identical. But as the weeks and months went on, reports grew detailed, more confident in their findings. Robert Hurd was mentally insane, and had developed an obsessive fascination with guns and violence. He had a toxic relationship with his mother, and had been bullied at school. He had no friends, no ambitions, no employment and no meaningful relationships.

The protective sibling within me jumped to my brother's defence. Charlie had friends, well maybe just Adam but he still counted. Charlie had ambitions, he wanted to go to art school. He had got accepted into Dundee School of Art, and he was scheduled to begin on the 16th of September, last year. He worked as a newspaper boy for a couple of summers, even though he hated it, and he did have a meaningful relationship – with me. I meant something to him. He meant something to me. I would've done anything for him. I could've helped him. Why didn't he let me help him?

Slamming the last plastic-protected newspaper closed, I clenched my jaw tight until I felt a sharp ache in the sides of my face. Tears stung my eyes, but I didn't let them fall. Not again. Taking a deep breath, I reminded myself why I had made this journey. Placing the newspapers gently back inside the 1987–1988 titled container, I slid the heavy box onto the shelf.

Sneaking past the huddle of elderly women at the sign-out desk, I exited through the same doors I came in. Crossing over, I followed the river trail to Sagamore Forest – the scene of the first shooting. Using the blotchy map I had created on a paper towel from the library bathroom, I retraced each fatal, gruesome, violent step.

From the forest, I walked to the petrol station in town then onto Hurd's reported place of residence. The street was long, but his house was easy to spot. Sandwiched between two equally burned-through brick houses was the charcoaled home of Robert Hurd. Although it had almost been burned to the ground by Robert's hands, it looked like no one had bothered to refurbish it for selling. They knew, like me, that a home this cursed would never sell. I just wished my parents would understand that.

From the condemned house, I walked towards the town common and then through the neighbouring streets where many had lain injured or dead. My finger grazed the mossy tips of the stone wall where a man had fallen, after throwing himself onto his wheelchair-bound wife to shield her from the bullets. They had both died.

Every house, every street, every stop on my journey revived old memories. Not just the ones of the days surrounding the Pembrook Academy shooting, but of the months and years before that. I couldn't breathe. My chest tightened, and panic seized my body, taking control. I knelt down, my hands sprawled out on the cold wet pavement. Light rain hit my fingertips and trickled between them, seeping onto the ground below. When the air came back, I collapsed onto the ground and leaned against the stone wall. Tipping my head back until I felt the coldness of the rain on my face, I sucked in deep desperate breaths. I felt my chest expand and contract, and slowly felt the throbbing in my head fade.

Panic attacks were becoming too common now. I would need to tell Dr Albreck about them – if she still allowed me therapy visits after my outburst. The frantic beating of my heart softened, and I eventually pulled myself up to standing. I had one more stop before my train back.

My journey through Hurd's eyes stopped at the place where the violence finally ended. The town's community college was Hurd's last location and where he had attended as a student. It was there, inside a technology classroom, that he took his own life. He had died in the place that had served as an educational institute preparing the next generation for a meaningful and prosperous life. Maybe there were similarities between Charlie and Robert Hurd. Maybe those comparisons would be my undoing.

'Horrible, isn't it?'

I slowly turned around and saw an older man, in a navy quilted raincoat walking his dog. 'What?'

'What happened here, I mean. Horrible, isn't it?' he said again, gesturing towards the building.

'I wouldn't know. I wasn't here at the time.'

'Count your blessings then.'

'Were you here?'

'I lived up on Ellon Avenue, by the church. I moved, after the shootings, to a smaller house near the river. One of my neighbours was killed in the attack, and it just got too hard seeing her house sit empty for so long. She was a lovely woman. Her daughter got shot in the leg, survived OK but moved away with her dad shortly after. Many people did. The town's not quite the same. A bit like Pembrook, I imagine. Tragedy follows tragedy.'

My throat got smaller, and when I swallowed it hurt.

'You probably don't know much about that either. Kids don't read newspapers or watch the news these days. It's all videogames and TV.'

'You'd be surprised at how much I know about Pembrook,' I said, before quickly adding, 'I watch the news with my dad.'

'All sounds a bit too familiar, if you ask me,' he said, shaking his head. 'Pointless deaths, all of them.'

'I hope you don't mind me asking, but did you know Robert Hurd?'

'Don't hear his name spoken much around here any more. But no, I don't mind. I knew his mother, not him so much. She worked at the school round the corner. Lovely lady. Had lost her husband two years before that, Robert's dad. I don't think he'd quite got over that. She talked a bit about how her son liked to keep to himself, didn't enjoy much company. She said she worried about him because he couldn't keep a job, was living with her and seemed distant.'

'How so?' I asked.

'Spent a lot of time in his bedroom alone, or out in the garden target shooting with Coke cans. When he did talk to her, he talked mostly about the end of the world. He was a loner. Impulsive. A deep-thinker, but not quite with it, you know?'

'Maybe he just needed someone to talk to, like a therapist or ... a relative.'

The old man shrugged, and rested a hand on the dog's head. The dog's tail sped up under his touch. I knelt down, and the dog pushed its wet nose into my face. I laughed, and held my hand out for balance. 'What's her name?'

'Millie. She's a good girl,' he smiled, patting her chest. 'What's your name?'

'Dougie,' I said, standing up and shoving my hands into my pockets nervously.

'Well, Dougie. It's been nice talking with you. I'm Joe. I'll probably see you around the town. You better get home before your parents start to worry, it's almost suppertime.'

The train ride home was much faster than the journey there, but that could've been because I was dreading going home. My parents wouldn't be worrying. They wouldn't have even noticed that I was gone. But more importantly, I hadn't got the answers I wanted. I didn't exactly know what I wanted, but I knew I hadn't succeeded in my objective. I wasn't any closer to finding Charlie's motive, to knowing what he was thinking in the moments before he turned the gun on himself and to excusing myself from the guilt and blame I had placed upon me and my family a long time ago.

Chapter 17

'Say Yes' *(Elliott Smith, Spring 1997)*

In the run-up to the national vote, media professionals got more vicious with their reports. Articles circulated describing an unhealthy relationship between Charlie and my dad. Mum was labelled as a hysterical shut-in, which wasn't entirely inaccurate just now. Then Dad became an abusive alcoholic who beat Charlie and drove him to violence. After reports about my family grew thin, newspapers turned to distant relatives, school bullying incidents, and finally circled back around to substance abuse.

But after my visit to Hurd's town, I knew now that this was a pattern. I had read countless newspaper articles that morning, each outlining one more detail. The media moves the population through a series of progressive emotional stages. First, shock. Then, sadness, confusion, remorse, anger. All culminating in the phase I was most looking forward to: closure. Readers move on to the next big story, the next tragedy. That's what the newspapers did with Robert Hurd. I just needed to hold on for a little longer. Then it would all be over. There were only so many headlines newspapers could create and even less that people could read. I just had to hold on.

I was still grounded from writing the letters to the families without my parents' knowledge or permission. Unfortunately, other than school, the only place I was allowed to leave the house for was Dr Albreck's office. That I couldn't miss, according to Dad, because I was the crazy one in the family, apparently.

When I got to Albreck's office, I pushed open the door and sighed. I just couldn't face her today. Heading for the chair in the corner where I always sat, I slumped down and waited for her. But as I flicked through a copy of *Home and Garden*, wondering whether Dr Fraser ever took my advice and managed to resuscitate his plant, the door creaked open, gaining my attention. Standing, or more correctly, sitting in the doorway was a student I recognised from Pembrook Academy. Peter something. But instead of the tall boy that I was used to seeing walking down the corridors, was a hunched-over figure in a wheelchair. I had read about him in the newspaper in the weeks after the shooting. He'd been hit in the spine by a stray bullet and was left permanently paralysed. I hid my face behind the magazine, terrified that he'd already seen me. He had.

'Sam?'

Slowly lowering the magazine, I peered over it and pretended to act surprised at seeing him. 'Oh, hi Peter.'

'Hey,' he said, coming closer to me. He paused and shook his head. 'Wow. It's so weird seeing you after so long, especially here.' He wheeled a tiny bit closer to me, close enough that I could see his palms were slightly calloused from constantly driving the rubber wheels.

'You come here?'

'It's only my third visit. My mum and dad thought it would be good for me. I've kinda been having a tough time lately. I didn't think this was permanent,' he said, motioning to the wheelchair.

'Is it?' I asked, putting the newspaper down in the empty seat beside me.

'Yeah, looks like it.' He smiled but his jaw was clenched, and his eyes looked vacant. The way Charlie used to smile, like he wasn't quite there.

'Sorry,' I whispered, once again wanting the ground to swallow me up and never release me.

'You've got nothing to be sorry about, Sam,' he said, gently slapping my arm, like we were football buddies out on the field. 'So, who are you here to see? I see Dr Fraser. He's OK, keeps trying to be my best friend though. Creeps me out a little,' he laughed.

Why was he being so nice to me? He should hate me, hate the sight of me. He was supposed to play pro football. And now he never would. But instead of screaming at me or ignoring me, he was chatting to me as if nothing happened, as if my brother hadn't shot him in a rage and left him without functional legs, without a future.

Instead of matching his kindness and treating him with the truth, I lied to him. 'I'm not here to see anyone,' I said, standing up and getting my coat on. 'I was just waiting for someone.' I started towards the waiting room exit. 'It was great to see you, Peter. You look ... good.'

I turned around and hurried through the double doors, almost tripping on the stairs. I needed to leave right that second. I couldn't breathe. I needed air. When I got outside, I leaned against the brick wall and breathed heavily, feeling the air enter and leave my lungs. I felt so guilty. He was waiting for me to confirm why I was in that waiting room, to affirm his reasons for also being there. But yet I couldn't admit that I needed help, like he did. I couldn't say the words. I was ashamed of needing help. I shouldn't need it. I wasn't the victim. I was part of the reason why he was going to be stuck in that chair his whole life.

I ran all the way home, my thighs burning and throbbing. When I got home, I slammed the door shut and leaned against it. Closing my eyes, I tried to force out the image of Peter in the wheelchair from my mind. But I couldn't. Hearing the arguing from upstairs, I moved towards it rather than away, needing to distract myself from my own thoughts. But when I got closer to their bedroom, I regretted listening in.

'He was depressed! He needed us!' screamed my mother, from behind the wooden door. I pressed my ear against it, needing more.

'You don't know what he needed! That's the truth – no one really knew what was going on inside that boy's head.'

'I knew. He told me – '

' – What did you say?'

'I said, I knew.'

'No, after that. You said, 'he told me'. He talked to you? When?'

'The night before.'

'Jesus, Linda. Why didn't you ever tell me?'

I could hear the slumping of a body down on the bed and the rustling of the quilt underneath, and knew my dad was sitting down.

'What did he say?' my dad asked.

'It was an odd interaction. First, he said things at school had got "worse".'

'What do you mean "worse"? Was he getting bullied?'

'Charlie preferred his paintbrushes to people, and Sam – '

' – Sam too?'

'They didn't fit in. Sam was always so preoccupied with his music and his books that I don't think he ever noticed. But Charlie, he notices everything. He was always like that, even as an infant. Do you remember? He would always know when we had been fighting, no matter how hard we pretended to be happy. He was so sensitive and empathetic. He felt everything. That's not normal eighteen-year-old behaviour. He was different from the rest of the boys at school, and he knew that. They knew that.'

'But he had friends.'

'He had Adam. That's it. Have you met Adam?'

'Yeah, weird kid… oh, Jesus. I can't believe I just said that. Was Charlie … weird?'

'No, Dan. Just different.'

'Tell me what else he said. Tell me everything.'

'He said some strange stuff about how colour isn't technically real, that it's a neurological side-effect of our brains trying to make sense of the overwhelming amount of visual information they take in.'

'What? What does that mean?'

'I don't know. That's just what he said. That was actually the last thing he said before he hugged me and went up to bed.'

'He hugged you?'

'I told you it was an odd interaction.'

'Do you have any idea of what you've done?'

I could hear my dad rising and begin to pace around.

'What *I've* done?'

'Your son comes to you the night before he decides to shoot up his school with an illegally acquired gun, and you dismiss it as "an odd interaction"?'

'I didn't dismiss it! I listened to him, something you've never done!'

'Did you listen to him, really? Because to me, it sounds like the desperate cries for help before a teenager is about to do something he'll regret. You could have stopped this!'

'How? Tell me, please, because I've replayed this conversation in my head every day since it happened. If you're such an expert on our son, who you barely talked to, then tell me what I could have done differently!'

'You could have told me!'

'Why? Because you were so involved in the parenting of our children?'

'Linda – '

' – Don't you dare blame me! I know the part I played in all of this, which is more than I can say for you. I know I'm guilty, but what about you?'

It sounded like a closet door swinging open and hitting the wall.

'Oh, that's right – walk away! That's what you're good at, Dan!'

The bedroom door swung open, and suddenly my dad was standing in the doorframe wearing his navy jacket and holding his wallet in his hand. He looked shocked to see me and opened his mouth to say something, but then closed it and slid past me quietly. A few moments later I heard the front door slam and the roaring of his car engine.

I peered around the frame and saw my mother sitting on the edge of the bed with her hands over her face. Her back shook as she leaned over, pressing her face deeper into her palms. I contemplated saying something, but like my dad I quietly slid away.

I heard her sobs throughout the night and every time I considered comforting her, I reminded myself that she didn't comfort my brother. And when morning came, when the sun rose from the horizon, I felt a new emotion stirring within me. Anger. Hatred. I was angry with my mother and blamed her, even though I knew there was nothing she could have done. And I didn't know whether I was so angry because I felt that she could have done something, or because I was jealous and somewhat hurt that Charlie chose to confide in her the night before, and not me.

And as I lay in bed, ignoring the alarm clock that buzzed beside me, new questions floated in front of me. Was he watching us run around trying to piece together his life, which seemed to be one complex puzzle? Did he ever intend for us to really know who he was and what he was thinking? Who was this stranger that I lived with for sixteen years?

Chapter 18

'Halo' *(Texas, Spring 1997)*

I saw Dougie in the corridor today. He pretended not to notice me and walked right by. I know he noticed me because his eyes flickered slightly to the side before swiftly returning to his target – the cafeteria door. I toyed with the notion of saying hello out loud but when I saw that eye flicker, 'hello' just seemed insufficient, maybe even insulting. I knew what I did was wrong, but it had happened and I couldn't change that. And honestly, I didn't know if I would want to. I was sorry for how it went down but I wasn't sorry for kissing her. And I never would be.

He didn't love Izzy. He loved the idea of her – carefree, trendy, whatever that means. I, on the other hand, didn't like the idea of her at all – rebellious, not confident in herself, pretending to be someone else – but I loved her. I loved the freckles on her nose, the birthmark on her left ear, the way she scrunched up her nose when she found something funny, and the snort that accidentally slipped out when she found something really funny. I bet if someone asked him Dougie couldn't tell you what Izzy dreamt about the night before, what her favourite Christmas present was, and what she used to bake with her mum. I could. Flying, probably – she always had flying dreams – a mint-green bike with a white bushel basket, and rainbow-dyed cookies. No, if you asked him Dougie could name what her favourite Mazzy Star song was or maybe, her alcohol preference for a Friday Frenzy. But he didn't know about her childhood memories of her mum or her affinity for chemical dyes in cookies. He didn't know her. I did. And the more I told myself that, the less guilt filled my mind and my thoughts.

But it was the way that Izzy looked at me in the cafeteria that brought the guilt crashing back down. The innocent half-smile that verged on condescension, and the exaggerated public display of affection told me that I was in this alone. Maybe I didn't know her after all.

'Sam Macmillan?'

Eyes blinking in surprise at having someone address me, I stared up at the hard lines forming around the boy's jawline. I already knew that this was not going to be a conversation that would start a budding friendship.

Sighing, I prepared myself for what was to surely come. 'Yes? What do you want to say?'

'I was asked to come find you. Your dad's here.'

'My dad? Where?' I said, glancing around.

'He's in the office with Ms Bevins.'

Feet slapping against the freshly mopped tile floor, I heard my steps echoing against the empty walls, void of student art or framed certificates of excellence. At Pembrook, glass displays encased trophies, awards and old rugby uniforms worn by those who graduated and moved on to coaching or pro leagues. My brother's painting of a seagull hovering over the bay hung next to the rest of his year's exam projects on the wall outside the art room. My brother had a talent and it was celebrated. So why did he hate the institution that recognised and celebrated that talent?

As I got closer to the office, sounds of anger and frustration suddenly seeped out from the thin walls like leaking rainwater. I immediately recognised my dad's voice. He didn't sound happy. But at least he was out of the garage.

Slowly and cautiously, I pushed open the office door and saw my dad standing with his back to me waving his arms.

'This is illegal, you know. You can't just suspend a student for no reason! I'll fight this!'

'Mr Macmillan, I already told you it's not a

suspension. For the safety of the other students, I thought it would be best to keep Sam at home. At least until after the vote when the media circus dies down. This isn't easy for us either ...' She stopped talking when she saw me standing there. Her expression was indecipherable. Was she scared of me? Did she feel sorry for me?

'Dad?'

He spun around. 'Sam, there you are. Get your bag. We're going home.'

'Why?'

'Truthfully, I don't know. But it seems people are too scared to have an opinion any more,' he yelled back at the office staff, who whispered under their breaths.

Chanting flowed through the building into the office even though the windows were closed tight. I wandered over to the glass and curiously looked out, as I heard my dad mutter profanities at the headteacher. Somehow between morning attendance and lunchtime, the amount of protesters outside had tripled. Wooden posts were staked into the grass, clumps of soil pooling around their bases as dozens of feet marched around them. Banners in enlarged font pressed against the windows as people outside recognised my face at the glass. The last words I saw before a secretary rushed over to lower the blinds were the posters, 'Vote Yes!' and 'Help the mentally unstable by voting tomorrow'.

'Sam, get away from the glass!' barked my dad as he continued his ranting, talking about bullying teenagers and unfair suspensions.

Mentally unstable. Was that my brother? Was he the mentally unstable in this spectacle outside? I was still getting over the drug accusations, possible depression and the comparisons to Robert Hurd. Him being psychologically unwell changed everything. Again.

'Dad, was Charlie – '

' – Sam, I told you get your stuff. We're leaving.'

Bag in hand, shoulders twitching, legs like jelly, I followed Dad as he pushed open the doors and met the sea of protesters who seemed to know the timing of our exit before we did. The crowd moved in closer, their chants getting louder, more aggressive.

'What's happening?' I yelled over the noise.

'The vote's tomorrow, and campaigning is getting out of control. I had to call the police to get them off the garden. That's our house!'

'Is this happening all over town?'

'Parts of Knightsbridge are closed off and Pembrook is mobbed right now. I could barely get through the streets. They're outside schools, libraries, down on the High Street – '

' – After tomorrow, will it finally be over?' My dad didn't respond, so I asked him again, this time louder. 'Dad, will it be over?'

'I don't know, Sam. I just don't know. I haven't exactly been truthful with you. The past few weeks have been bad. Your letters didn't help much either.'

'Bad? Or worse?'

'I threw out two huge black bags of hate mail last night, someone threw another brick through our window, and your mum had a rough time at the shops this morning.'

'What happened?'

'Someone spat in her face in the dairy aisle. Got her all upset,' he said, digging around for his car keys.

'Dad, they're coming this way,' I said, pointing to the crowd walking over to us.

'Our faces are on every newspaper around the country and the news channels have been broadcasting CCTV footage of the shootings. It's like it's happening all over again,' he said, as he finally dug out his keys. 'Well, don't just stand there. Get in the car.'

Throwing my bag into the back seat of my dad's Fiat, I plopped down in the passenger seat and slammed on the radio to drown out the noises outside the car and inside my head. 'Am I expelled?'

'No, of course not. But you can't return for the next few days. They're calling it a scheduled leave of absence, although I don't know who scheduled it. I certainly didn't know about it until an hour ago.' He shifted into gear and reversed back, sending me flying forwards. 'Look at this. They're everywhere. Move!' He honked the horn and revved his engine. 'I'll run you all over!' Eventually the sea parted, and an exit route was found.

'Where's mum?' I asked, realising that Dad's presence in situations like this was rare. His breath also didn't smell of beer for once. He looked revved up, present, and more importantly, involved.

'She ... not home,' he answered, his eyes moving to the rear-view mirror.

'There's no one behind us,' I reassured him. 'What do you mean she's not home? Where is she?'

'She took a train down south to your Aunt Jackie's.'

'Because of what happened this morning at the shops?'

'Because she's sick of the photographers outside our house and – I tell you this because you're not a kid any more, Sam – things haven't been good between us for a while now and she's had enough.'

'And when you say 'for a while', you mean since June?'

'Your mum says I've changed.'

'We've all changed! Who wouldn't come out different in a situation like this? She's changed too – she's still cleaning her dead son's room and buying his favourite Pop Tarts, for God's sake!'

'Language, Sam.'

'This is bullshit!'

'Sam! Language!'

The car pulled into the driveway, my dad having driven at least fifteen miles over the limit the entire way, knowing no policeman would dare try to pull him over at this moment. I flung open the door, leaving my bag in the car, and raced into the house and upstairs.

'Sam, come down!'

'Why? Mum gets to check out, why can't I?'

Fury taking over my body, blood burning in my veins, I launched into my room. The radio was still on from the morning, blasting news about the vote and last year's shootings. When would it end? 'Leave us alone!' I screamed, yanking the cord out of the socket. Chest heaving, I hoisted the radio onto the window frame and watched as it soared down to the driveway and exploded into metal fragments.

'Sam? What the hell was that?'

Slamming the window shut, I huddled under the ledge and tucked my legs in under my chin. Hugging myself tight, I squeezed my eyes shut and tried to remember Izzy's crooked smile, her freckled nose, her green eyes that shimmered with flecks of amber. But no matter how hard I tried to picture her face, the only person that appeared before me was my brother.

Chapter 19

'Let Down' *(Radiohead, Spring 1997)*

It was scarcely light outside when I finally came to, a distant bell ringing in the background. My body was slumped against the wall, my head resting awkwardly on the CD rack beside me. Had I fallen asleep? Fainted? What time was it?

A ringing echoed through the dark house, waking me up and bringing me back. Leaning on the bedside table, I hoisted my heavy body up and steadied myself. For a moment, I wondered where my black clock radio was. The thick silver dust outlined a clean rectangular shape on the table where it once sat. Then I remembered.

Feeling my body get heavy again, I staggered over to the bed and crawled in under the quilt like an insect searching for a cool dark place to hide. Curling my body inwards, I hugged my knees to my chest and felt my back spasm as I suppressed a sob that bubbled inside. I couldn't do this. I couldn't go on like this. I couldn't take any more. I squeezed my eyes tight until my eyelids hurt, and wished that I would never wake up again. Even though the room was silent, loud noises filled my head. My hands gripped my ears, but I couldn't block out the sounds. They were inside me.

As I slowly drifted in and out of consciousness, the noises faded and in their place were the murmurings of Charlie's voice. His whisperings guided me into a slumber so deep that my body sank heavily into the mattress and didn't move an inch until I opened my eyes several hours later.

When I awoke, I saw that my bedroom door was slightly ajar. My body felt stiff and ached as I stretched it out. Pulling the covers off me, a cool blast of air washed over me and I gulped hungrily. A deep muffled voice echoed up the stairs and seeped in through the opening in my door, tempting me out of hiding.

Breaths heavy and drawn out, I slowly inched down the stairs. The flickering of the television set reflected off the kitchen counter. Swirls and flashes of red, green and black shone onto the white tiles. I could hear my dad talking, and when I peered around the corner, I saw the phone cord that snaked around the armchair and wound up to my dad, who sat with his back to me.

'Linda, just come home ... I'm not the only

guilty one here ... that's not fair ... come on ... and what about Sam? You know I can't look after him all by myself. I don't know how to take care of the boy. He's upstairs trashing furniture ... no, no he's fine ... I didn't do anything to him. You're the one who left! He's angry with you, not me! Linda? Hello?'

He placed the receiver back on the base, and sighed loudly. Then he straightened up as if he knew someone was watching him. 'Sam, is that you?'

I took a deep breath. It began. 'Yeah.'

'You owe me a clock radio.'

'Yeah.' I sulked into the living room, expecting some yelling, throwing of TV or VCR controls and possibly even a punch to the wall. But they never came. My dad looked tired, heavy circles outlining his defeated eyes. He gestured toward the other end of the sofa.

I dropped down, the fabric softening and hugging my body. We'd had that sofa since I was small, and it had weathered spillages, stains, tantrums, naps and the occasional 'circus jump'. It was old and comfortable, and I liked the way it remembered my body when I sat in it. I looked over at Dad who was rubbing his forehead, the way my brother used to when he was stressed. 'Was that Mum?'

'I didn't intend for you to hear that.'

I slid further down in the sofa, until my head rested against the top cushion. 'Is she coming home?'

'I don't know. I never know what goes on inside her head. She barely talks to me.'

I laughed at the irony, then quickly bit down on my lip when I saw my dad staring at me. A thunderous bang from the hallway startled me, and I sat upright.

'Relax, it's just the post.'

'Should I go get it?'

'No,' he said, his fingers barely moving as he skipped the channels on the TV, as if searching for something.

'What time is it?' I asked, rubbing the sleep from my eyes.

'Almost eight o'clock in the morning.'

'I've never slept that long before.' I turned around to face him and saw him staring at the TV, his eyes glued on the images and the headlines that moved from right to left across the screen. 'It's today, isn't it?'

My dad nodded, but didn't look away from the TV.

'Are you going to the polling station?'

No response.

'You can't just sit here all day staring at that thing. It'll drive you crazy. We should turn it off.'

He shivered slightly and swallowed bitterly, as if his throat burned.

'Dad?'

Taking the cue, I turned around and trudged up the stairs back to my prison cell. But instead of seeking out the cool secure cocoon that my bed offered, I stretched out on my bedroom floor. Lying on my back, I gazed up at the tiny stars on my ceiling. Some had peeled off, while others had curling edges. In the six years that had followed that day, a lot had happened. Our adolescent years had gradually created a distance between my brother and me.

We had always been close and still were right up to the end, but suddenly afternoons looking at comics together or Saturday mornings watching *Scooby Doo* cartoons were replaced with solitary periods in our respective rooms. For Charlie, his focus turned to art and for me, piano practice occupied most of my free time. Any time left was dedicated to the stack of books that sat next to my bed frame on the floor. Jack Kerouac, John Steinbeck, Harper Lee and Ernest Hemingway captured my attention and soon those evenings spent huddled around the television set drinking hot cocoa with Charlie were spent in my bedroom, alone. We grew up. We got older. We became too much like our father. We lost what it meant to be a family. We all lived under the same roof, but the walls we'd built around us divided us in many ways. We were like a broken vase – long before Charlie walked into Pembrook that morning – we could glue the pieces back together, but the cracks would always be visible. And no matter how hard anyone tried, we'd always be damaged.

Even though it was daytime and the stickers no longer glowed in the dark, the stars burned bright in my eyes, so bright that I had to look away. Sitting up, I curled my body in and rested my chin on my knees. Squeezing my eyes shut, I slowly began counting down from 100. Dr Albreck recommended using the counting as a way of 'calming the mind' and 're-establishing control.' She told me to count backwards from 20, but every time I did that my mind was still racing and my head pounded. So, I chose 100. When I got down to 40, I felt my shoulders relax slightly and the lump in my throat vanish. By the time I landed on 20, my hands were planted on the floor and I was rising to stand. After today, this would be all over. I hoped.

Edging back down the stairs, I stopped in the hallway and gathered the mail in my arms. Letting it spill out on the kitchen counter, my eyes gazed at the newspaper headline: 'How a small-town school shooting led to the country's biggest vote.'

Sliding into a bar stool, I leaned over the counter absorbing every word. A six-page special listed everything from a detailed account of the day of the shootings to families' anguished memories of that fatal morning. Those who died got at least half a page dedicated to celebrating their academic and personal achievements. I had no idea that Cara Johnson was training for the London Marathon, or that Geoff Linders volunteered at the local elderly home on weekends. I didn't know them at school, and now I was learning about them after death. I wondered if Charlie knew anything about them, other than their social status at school. Did he know that Andrew Edwards' sister was battling leukaemia? Or did Charlie only focus on the fact that he was on the rugby team and therefore just as guilty of bullying and ostracism as his team members?

The boy in the wheelchair from Dr Albreck's office was in there too. Peter Owen. He seemed to have a smaller article because he'd survived. But his story was in there. I guess he was only three weeks out from beginning his professional league football career. He was to move down south and begin training with the club who'd signed him. The newspaper touted the young player as the next David Beckham. A sharp ringing from the living room startled me. The piercing sound sent shivers deep into my bones. 'Dad, are you going to answer that?' I called out, turning the pages of the newspaper slowly.

'Probably just reporters again. I'm not giving them the satisfaction of answering their calls!'

The ringing continued. 'It might be Mum,' I said, closing the paper. I heard his body quickly move from the sofa and a muffling of his voice as the ringing ended.

'Sam, it's for you.'

'Who is it?'

'A girl from school. Izzy?'

I pushed the paper away from me, sliding it across the smooth surface until it hit the edge of the counter and stopped. 'Tell her I'm not here.'

The phone rang after that, and again after that, until Dad finally disconnected it from the wall. Then, it was just us and silence. I didn't know whether Izzy was calling again, or Mum, or whether all the phone calls were from reporters hungry for a statement on Vote Day. We would never find out, and that was just fine with me.

The morning dragged on into the afternoon, and Dad fought the urge to turn the TV back on until after the polls were in. We closed our curtains, turned off the lights and lit only a few candles around us. We ignored the occasional knock on the door and blocked out the rare verbal exchange outside our house regarding the voting. We didn't want to know what the country was doing, or deciding. For that small amount of time, we wanted to shut out everything and remain invisible until a verdict had been reached, and the future taken out of our hands.

While Dad disappeared into the garage, I curled up on the living-room floor in front of a blank TV screen reading the six-page newspaper special over and over. Soon the words were a part of me, and me a part of them. My eyes got heavy and my body sank slowly into the soft carpet, my head landing on the black-and-white paper. The last image I saw before I drifted off was the smiling face of one of Charlie's victims.

When I came to, flashes and flickerings of colour hit my eyes as my lids slowly opened. Sluggishly, I sat up and leaned against the sofa. My dad sat in the armchair on the other side and didn't acknowledge my awakening. His eyes were fixed on the TV. Images of massed crowds filled the screen, and underneath flashed the headline, 'The impact of Yes.'

That was it. Yes. People had decided. Charlie's actions had bled out into politics and history. The day had passed too quickly, the vote almost too easy. But no one knew as much as me how uneasy this had all been. Amidst the poll review of how votes were counted and which geographical areas were split, reports of weapon donations flooded in. All across the country, people in possession of arms were voluntarily stepping forward and handing in their weapons. Not just handguns, this vote had prompted the population to reconsider private ownership of any kind of weapon. Licensed semi-automatic pistols, rimfire rifles, shotguns and Glocks were being dropped off at police stations across the country. In 24 hours, 162,000 weapons and 700 tons of ammunition would have been handed in. For many, that day would signify community and solidarity. For me, I would remember it as the day the fog finally lifted, and my life recommenced.

Chapter 20

'It's No Good' *(Depeche Mode, Spring 1997)*

When I awoke that morning, I spent my initial moments jotting down fragments of my dream. On the page was a single drawing of a beating heart. I didn't know who it belonged to in my dream. Around the heart, I scribbled words and short phrases detailing other images from my dream: my brother's easel, my dad's watch, Izzy's face. Separately, those things held many meanings – unnecessary loss, the passing of time, love. But together, I didn't know what they meant. All I knew was that those things were all I remembered from my dream the night before.

Sliding the pencil and journal back into the bottom drawer of my bedside table, I noticed how full it had become. What had started as a trivial activity to document and express emotions I couldn't understand, had now become a daily ritual treasured as the most important part of my journey this year. More surprisingly, deep dark lines and angry scribbles had turned into the occasional harmony and note, creating my own music sheet of emotions. I was thinking about music again. I was dreaming about music again. I was getting better, stronger. Maybe I would get through this after all.

Swinging the covers off my bed, I marched over to my closet and threw my upper body into the clutter that had built up on the floor. From the stacks of clothes, books and incomplete homework assignments, I found the edge of my music box.

Sliding the box towards me, I slid off the lid and reached my hand in. It grazed the top of music sheets, books on harmony, and visuals for both the major and minor scales. The paper felt familiar to my touch. Grabbing a stack of paper, I dropped it into my lap and began flicking through the pages. I quickly found the paper-clipped solo pieces that I'd intended to outline on my free-choice programme in the application pack for the Royal Academy of Music in London. The audition was what I'd been working on right before the shootings. I'd read the requirements over and over, and could relay by memory what was expected of me and what was at stake.

I'd already listed eight solo pieces, and highlighted the one that I really wanted to perform – 'All the Things You Are'. It was jazz, and likely not up to the Academy's concerto standards. But I knew it by heart, and more importantly, really loved to play it. Charlie loved to listen to it. It was his favourite. He said, every time he listened to it, it inspired a new painting. He could have just been saying that, but I liked playing it for him.

A heavy feeling sunk in my belly. I'd missed the audition. I'd been here, dealing with all this. Playing 'All the Things You Are' on the piano had been the last thing on my mind. And now I'd missed my only chance to get into the Royal Academy of Music. My only chance to move away from here and really start afresh.

I scooted over to my dad's old turntable that I'd borrowed several years ago and not yet given back. Sliding the vinyl out, I placed it gently on top and swung the needle over it. The song flowed out, the vinyl spinning around slowly. There it was. My song. Charlie's song. Leaning back, I lay on the floor and gazed up at the star stickers again, listening to every chord played and every word sung. The piano was barely detectable, but pulling the notes out and performing them entirely on the piano was really something. That was the song to me, not this.

'I thought I heard you,' said my mum, peering around the door.

I sat up quickly, and leaned over to turn off the music.

'No, leave it,' she said, hovering in the doorway. Her face was red, puffy and she looked older, haggard with age and sadness. Her auburn hair fell just above her shoulders, slightly wavy at the ends.

'When did you get here?'

'Just a few minutes ago. Can I come in?'

I gestured towards the bed with the vinyl sleeve still in my hand. She moved from the doorway, and slowly walked towards the bed, sitting on the covers. She looped her fingers together nervously and rested them in her lap. She didn't say anything.

'Are you back?' I asked.

'No, Sam. I'm not coming back. Your dad knows that.'

'I wish someone had told me.'

'Have you been reading the papers?'

'I thought it would die down after the vote, but it seems to be the same. Now I don't know when I'll be allowed to go back to school.'

'I'm sorry about school, but I don't believe it's going to be for long. Another week maybe, until the media find someone else to follow around. I don't blame Ms Bevins, really. It must be hard facing all those parents who don't want their children caught up in all of this.'

'Do you think they're scared of me? Of us?'

'I think they don't understand. And maybe they still blame us, but not you, Sam. We were Charlie's parents. It was our responsibility to protect you both, take care of you.' She shifted to the edge of the bed, but didn't rise to get up. 'I'm sorry. For everything. We really made a mess of things,' she said, her voice cracking at the end. Her bottom lip quivered and she placed her hand up to it as if she could steady it. 'But, it looks like we'll be able to move on soon. The house sold, finally.'

'Really? Who bought it?'

'A young couple – newlyweds – from down south. We lowered the price by a lot and we found someone desperate enough to take it. Not a great financial decision for your father and me, but it needed to be done.'

'So, what now?'

'Assuming the sale goes through, your dad will look for a job and a house for the two of you. I guess it all depends on your plans for after you've finished school.'

'So you won't be coming with us,' I added, nodding as if I had known from the moment she knocked on my bedroom door.

'I want to, believe me.'

'Then what is it?'

'I'm not doing well,' she said, running her hand through her hair. Her hand dropped heavily back into her lap. 'I'm having a hard time getting through this, Sam. And that's not easy for me to admit.'

'We're all having a hard time, Mum. That's why you sent me to a therapist.'

She opened her mouth like she was about to say something, but then closed it and straightened up slightly. 'I haven't heard you play this song in a while.'

'I haven't wanted to play it in a while, but recently I've felt different,' I admitted.

'Yeah, these past couple of months have really been the turning point for us.'

My eyes shot up to meet hers. Turning point. Just like Dr Albreck had said. The vote – that was our turning point. Or had I already faced mine when I first met Izzy?

'I should get going. I just came to deliver the news of the sale.' She got up and slowly walked towards the door. 'Your father looks really good,' she added.

'Yeah, he's not drinking any more,' I shrugged.

She smiled. 'We really couldn't have survived this past year without you, Sam.'

'Mum?'

Her head popped back from behind the door. 'Yes?'

'Do you think it's too late to apply to the Royal Academy of Music for September?'

'I didn't realise you were still considering that. No, I don't think it's too late at all.'

'I probably won't get in even if there are spots left over. I haven't practised in months.' I scrunched my fingers inwards and stretched them back out, already feeling a considerable difference in strength and agility. My body felt old, strained.

'Then you better get practising,' she nodded, and shut the door behind her.

After she left, I crept downstairs and lifted the lid of the mahogany piano that sat in the corner of the dining room. Framed photos of Charlie and me lined the top of the piano. I smiled at the one of us pulling silly faces in the back garden. I took a deep breath, and started playing. And I played all afternoon, in my pyjamas and unwashed hair. I played until the grumbling in my belly got too loud to ignore, eventually coaxing me off the cushioned bench seat and into the kitchen.

My dad leaned against the counter, unfolding flat-packed cardboard boxes. 'I was wondering when you'd get back on that thing.'

'Packing already?' I said, sloppily putting together a peanut-butter sandwich.

'So, your mum told you?'

I nodded, stuffing a piece of bread into my mouth.

'If the buyers don't pull out, we'll soon be leaving Pembrook for good.'

A sharp pain shot across my chest. I had been

so eager for a fresh start that I hadn't thought about that – never returning to Pembrook. Charlie and I had lived in this house our whole lives. Red permanent marker still stained the doorframe where he'd signed his name. We would need to paint over that before we left.

Looking around I saw fragments of our lives all around me. The chip in the counter tile where he'd slammed a pot down during one of his arguments with Dad. The scratches in the hardwood flooring near the back door where he'd dragged his art easel out one evening to paint the sunset. The doodles on the fridge from the time we'd scribbled on it with permanent marker. We got grounded for that one.

My brother had existed in this space. Now it would be filled with someone else's furniture, someone else's memories. Tears stung my eyes, but I choked them back. We learned early on not to cry in front of Dad. He was from a different generation, a different culture. Boys didn't enjoy art classes. Boys didn't play musical instruments. And boys certainly didn't cry when they were sad.

When I glanced up, I saw Dad staring at me but I couldn't tell what he was feeling. I never could. With Mum gone, we just had each other now. We had never really spent that much time together. This was a new experience for him and me. One I didn't know we would enjoy. I didn't know anything about my dad. Most kids know what their dad does all day for work, what they like to do for fun, and even their favourite foods. But I didn't know anything about my dad. He had, intentionally I think, remained a complete mystery to everyone around him. And because of that I felt hugely guilty about the next stage of my life. Charlie had never had the opportunity to connect with Dad. He had never allowed it. And now here he was standing right in front of me – sober – promising me a future away from the town that was suffocating us. A future together. That was all Charlie ever wanted. He would never know Dad like I would.

'Sam, can I show you something?'

Scuffling slowly behind him, I followed him to the garage. I wavered at the doorway. I'd never been allowed in before.

'Come in,' he said, gesturing inwards.

Stepping over the lipped frame, my feet clumsily found the stairs in the semi-darkness. Dad leaned in and flicked the light switch. An amber glow enveloped us and illuminated everything around us. Immediately I saw what my dad was showing me, and knew why.

In the middle of the garage, on a raised platform was a wooden bench stained white. Not a crisp white, but a soft antique white. Walking over, I touched my hand to the wood. Shiny and smooth, the wood felt cold under my touch. A glimmer of silver caught my eye, and when I gazed up I saw a small oval plaque. Etched in the centre, in my father's handwriting, was my brother's full name. Charles Daniel Macmillan.

All those hours he had spent here, us thinking he was getting drunk in his failed woodman's workshop, and he was building this. It was a bench, crafted by my father for one sole purpose – to remember the son he'd lost.

I could only think of one thing. 'Has Mum seen this?'

He shook his head. Always concealing something, always hiding himself.

'If Mum saw this, she would understand. This is all she wants. This is all we ever wanted, Dad. To know you,' I said, my voice cracking.

And as if it had never happened, as if it were a dream, he turned off the lights and clouded us once again in his darkness.

Chapter 21

'The End is the Beginning is the End'
(Smashing Pumpkins, Summer 1997)

Day after day, evening after evening, I practised my audition pieces. When I wasn't avoiding Dougie and Izzy at school, I was at home playing the piano. Dad had packed up most of the house by the time my audition came around, thankfully not asking me for help. He knew I was preparing for something, but never asked me about it. Dad's interest in my passion for music fluctuated between minimal and non-existent. But I didn't mind. He showed me the bench in the garage, what he'd been working on all this time. We were making progress, and that was all that mattered.

The Academy got back to me having selected three pieces from my free-choice programme, including the one I wanted to play. They'd asked for an essay. I sent them two. One answered a question pertaining to modern musical arrangements. The second answered a question not even asked. In it, I talked about my year and what I'd learned from it. It was honest, devastating at times, but real. I knew they'd recognise my name from the papers and wonder, maybe even do their own research, so I wanted to create my own first impression. It somehow worked. They contacted me three weeks later explaining that although it wasn't exactly accredited prior or experiential learning, they recognised it was a year in which I'd experienced more than any of their students combined. They offered me an audition. To them, I was an applicant. To me, they were my life jacket.

I practised, and practised. And when my fingers ached and begged for a break, I practised some more. And then it was Audition Day. Mum drove me to the audition, and waited less than two hours in the car while I entered and exited.

'Well?' she asked, as I saddled into the passenger seat. My music sheet folder lay flat along the back seat, snuggled between cardboard boxes of her belongings taken from the house that morning. 'Sam? How did it go?'

'Fine.'

'You are exactly like your father. Tell me more. I've been sitting here since 10am this morning!'

'There was a man and a woman from the admissions office. They asked me to play the chosen pieces. So, I did. There's not much to tell. I don't know how I did.'

'So is that it?'

'I won't know anything for a couple of weeks. I'll get a letter in the post, they said.'

'You don't look very happy about it.'

I looped my fingers together in my lap, feeling the strain. 'I was nervous. I could have played better.' I ran my fingers through my hair, and clenched my jaw. I hadn't even expected an audition this late in the year, so why was I so disappointed?

My mum repositioned herself back into her seat and fastened her seatbelt. 'Well, it's done now and you can't go back. So, be proud that you did it. I know what will cheer you up – ice cream!'

'Mum, I'm sixteen – soon to be seventeen.'

'Seventeen-year-olds don't eat ice cream any more?'

I smiled. She was trying. Driving me here, waiting patiently in the car, now the ice-cream. This was strangely normal for a teenager – a mother trying hard to impress her teenage son when she knows he's grown up.

'Yeah, seventeen-year-olds eat ice cream. You pick the place,' I shrugged. I glanced back at the music sheet folder on the back seat. Maybe I should have reread the music sheets before going in there.

'Sam, you'll think you did worse than you did. Stop thinking about it.'

'I'm not thinking about the audition,' I said, looking out of the passenger window. I had been so consumed with the audition, I hadn't remembered what day it fell on. A woman pushed a pram, with a young girl walking beside her. She wore a red dress and gazed at me through the window. She looked around eight or nine years old. Did she know what day it was today?

I glanced back at Mum. She had a strange expression on her face. Her eyes were glistening, her cheeks slightly red. Did she know what day it was? Before I could figure out what she was thinking, what she was feeling, she shook the expression from her face and sighed gently. 'We'll remember today as the day you worked hard for your future, and not for anything else.' She smiled at me and affectionately gripped my shoulder. 'Now, let's get that ice cream.'

***

When we got back to the house, Izzy was waiting for me on the doorstep.

'Who's that?' asked my mum, pulling into the driveway.

'No one. Just a girl from school,' I said, glaring through the windscreen.

'She doesn't look like no one.'

Izzy stood up and walked towards the car. She looked different. Instead of her usual too-short skirt and too-cool shirt, she wore faded blue jeans and a simple white T-shirt that had little lace frills on the sleeves. Tucking her hair behind her ear, she smiled eagerly. 'Hi, Mrs Macmillan. I'm Isobel.' She waved awkwardly. Why was she so nervous?

'Hi, Isobel. Please call me Linda. Do you go to school with Sam?'

'Yes, we know each other from Knightsbridge. We have some classes together.'

'Mum, could you give us a minute?' I abruptly said, dismissing the painfully awkward interaction between the girl who broke my heart and my mother.

She nodded and headed into the house, glancing back several times before closing the front door.

'Hey, Sam.'

'Hey. What's going on? Why you here?'

'Because you've been avoiding me. And I wanted to see how you are. It's the anniversary of Pembrook, right?'

I didn't say anything. Nervously, I slid my hands into my pockets rubbing the sweat from my palms against the cotton lining.

'We haven't really had a chance to talk since winter. I've tried calling you, and I even came round to your house last month but no one answered. Anyway, I'm sorry that we haven't hung out since New Year's Eve. These past few months must have been awful. I didn't want that to happen. Even Dougie recognises that this was a shitty thing to do.' She paused, waiting for me to speak.

'No one has talked to me in six months. Six months! All because of a drunk kiss. I expected that from Dougie. You were his girlfriend. But you?'

'I know. I'm sorry for the way I acted after New Year's Eve. It was as much my fault as it was yours, yet I acted like you had totally misread the situation. The truth is I wanted to kiss you. I've wanted to kiss you for a while now, probably since I met you.'

'Why are you telling me this now? What about Dougie?'

'Dougie and I are over. I think he's seeing Noel's ex, which is not a smart move. I thought you knew. I called you right after – '

' – I get it. So, you get dumped and come running to me. Is this what you do?'

'No, I'm here because I want to be here.'

'You're here because you're alone and you don't know how to be alone.'

She took a step back, like someone had just punched her in the gut. I guess I had. 'You don't know anything about me, Sam,' she said, her voice barely a whisper.

'You're right. I don't. I don't know who the real you is. How could I? You're always pretending to be someone else. You were blonde fun-loving Izzy when you dated those guys from the year above. You were dark-haired, pierced punk Izzy when you dated Dougie. Who will you be with me? Will you start learning the piano? Become a classical music enthusiast? You have more sides to you than a hexagon!'

'This was a bad idea,' she said, marching past me.

I spun around, ready to call out her name, to stop her. But I couldn't. I was so angry at her. Not because we kissed and she pretended that it was all me, not because she went back to Dougie immediately after. But because she was my friend, and she wasn't there for me. I had never felt so alone, so depleted, and she was nowhere to be found. I was done. I was tired. I just wanted peace in my life. I knew that there were more girl dramas to come, but I was just exhausted and wanted nothing more than a simple, boring, normal life where nothing exciting happened.

After saying goodbye to my mum, and watching an awkward exchange of acknowledgement between her and my dad, I sat down to the anniversary

TV special that I'd promised myself I wouldn't watch. Gripping a cup of tea, I leaned into the TV, captivated by every frame. After a brief history of Pembrook and the school shootings, images filled the screen of a memorial garden erected where the assembly hall once stood. Hundreds of white roses encircled a stone monument with the names of those who had perished that day. And beside the rose garden was Princess Diana clutching a white candle, lit. She bowed her head and led a three-minute silence. And when that was over, she encouraged people all over the country to light a candle and remember the day our students had died.

And when the TV special ended, I went into the kitchen cabinet and took out a small votive candle. Striking the match carefully, I touched the tip to the wick and let the flames lick the air. Carrying the candle upstairs, I rested it on the windowsill in my brother's bedroom. And that night, as the candle flickered and sparked I gazed out of the window at the hundreds of candles that I saw in my neighbours' homes, out on the streets and along the road. That night, I dreamt of a calm ocean and a cool breeze that flowed through my hair and over my skin. That night, I didn't dream of death.

Chapter 22

'Staring at the Sun' (U2, Summer 1997)

The week before the formal dance, I decided to visit Izzy. I knocked on her door with a loud thump and waited for the murmured shuffling of feet as they approached the door. But when they opened it, I didn't see Izzy but I saw her small round nose and almond-shaped green eyes in the face that appeared.

'You must be Izzy's dad. I'm Sam,' I said, wondering if I should disclose my last name before asking for time alone with his daughter. 'Is Izzy home?'

Before he could respond, Izzy's delicate hands slid out around the door as she wrestled it out of her father's grasp. 'It's OK, Dad. I've got this.' He walked away, glancing back as he disappeared from the hallway. 'What do you want, Sam?'

'Do you want to go for a walk?'

'Why? I thought we said all we had to at your house?'

'Please, Izzy.'

She shut the door promptly, but reopened it with her coat in one hand. 'I have to be home in an hour. Carol's taking me out for dinner,' she said, sliding her arms into a light-green corduroy jacket that had the sleeves turned up exposing the edges of her greyish denim shirt underneath.

'Just the two of you? Really?' I smiled.

'Let's just say we've been spending a lot of time together this term, and she's not that bad.'

'That's great. I'm really happy for you.'

'It was about time. It's not her fault Mum died. I can't keep hating her forever.'

We took the trail near her house, which led into the woodlands behind Debbie's. The path turned muddy and the sky above vanished, the thick branches of the beech trees closing in around us. We walked a little of the way in silence, the only noises coming from our feet and the chirping of the birds above. Although it was already June, my bare arms shivered in the cool breeze.

'I'm really sorry for how things ended last time,' I said, keeping my eyes fixed on the ground beneath me.

'Me too. I never wanted to fight with you, Sam.'

'I was angry about a lot of things, and I took it out on you. I'm sorry.'

'Stop saying "Sorry". You say it too much.'

The woodlands got thicker, the silence around us almost peaceful. Suddenly she stopped walking and turned to me. 'Sam, I want you to know that my feelings for you were ... *are* real. I was never using you to get back at Dougie for cheating, or to annoy my dad and Carol. Or because I was bored. I would never have done that to you. I promise.'

'I never thought that.'

'But in case you did and you didn't want to tell me, I just wanted to say it first.' She grabbed my hand, and squeezed it. But I couldn't return her affections. I slid my hand out from hers and started walking again.

'I don't understand,' she said, jogging a couple of steps to catch up.

'That's not why I came here.'

'Then why did you come?'

' – I can't be your rebound, Izzy. I want more. I deserve more.'

'You're not my rebound,' she said, grabbing my arm to stop me walking. 'Don't you like me any more?'

'I ... I don't know.'

'You don't know?' she said, dropping her grasp.

'I just ... don't feel like myself. I don't know myself any more. I don't know what makes me happy.'

'And by that, you mean you don't know if *I'll* make you happy.'

I shrugged and slid my hands deep into my pockets, feeling the first drop of rain hit my nose. I glanced up at the sky, trying to see the dark clouds hovering above us.

'What do you want, Sam?'

When my eyes met Izzy's again, I saw that she was wiping a tear from her eye. 'I don't know,' I answered eventually.

'Take some time and figure out what you want. But I'm not going to wait around forever.' She walked away, heading back up the trail towards her house. Instead of following her, I kept on going down the path, deeper and deeper into the woods. When I reached the edge, the woodlands spilled out into an open field.

Rather than turning back, I knelt down on the ground bordering the field. My feet in the forest, my knees in the field, I let the air enter my lungs and pushed it out. We were to release Charlie's ashes in a few weeks. I never understood why people referred to emptying an urn of ashes as a Release. We weren't setting a caged animal free or pardoning a prisoner for his crimes. Or, were we?

I didn't move until the sun set low in the hills beyond the field and the dusky air of nighttime set in. My legs ached and burned, but soon loosened up as I neared the end of the woodland trail. I glanced back at Izzy's house and saw a light up in her bedroom. I wondered what she was doing.

When I got home, Dad was sitting at the kitchen counter. Cardboard boxes lay scattered around his feet, the tops taped down securely with beige masking tape.

'What are you doing?' I asked, sliding my feet out of my shoes.

'Just paying the last month of bills. Is your room packed up?'

'Dad, we're not leaving for another month.'

'It'll come up fast.'

I hovered near him while he wrote. 'Do you want to watch TV together? Maybe we can pick a movie?' The words felt foreign to me, but then again nothing would ever feel familiar again.

My dad frowned, like he was thinking hard about something, and stopped writing. He relaxed his grasp on the pen and it fell to the side of the paper. He opened his mouth to say something then closed it quickly. He picked up his pen and began scribbling again. 'No, I'm too busy but you go ahead.'

The next day, I sat on the same armchair that I always sat in and tilted my head to the window beside me and stared out, like I always did. But something about that session felt different, and not just because it was supposed to be my last therapy appointment. Everything felt different – the colours of the sky through the window, the sounds of the car engines from the streets below, even the collective sounds of our breathing patterns.

'Dr Albreck?'

'Yes?'

'What do you think drives someone to kill?'

'Sam, you've been seeing me for nearly a year and you've never asked me a question like that. Why would you ask me that now?'

'I thought coming here was a waste of time.'

'And now?'

'I tried to answer that question myself. I've been trying to answer it for months. And I don't feel any closer to knowing what happened.'

'Honestly, Sam, I don't think anyone really knows what drives people to kill. We're all exposed to the same violence we see on the news, in movies, even out in our streets. There is so much pain and loss in this world, yet only a handful of us are driven to kill.'

'The police found movies in my brother's bedroom – violent movies that he'd secretly bought. They said on the news that he'd watched one over and over again. Do you think they inspired him? Do you think he wanted to emulate them?'

'Violence we see on the TV is often cited as

the reason why teenagers are violent. Yes, you could argue that what we see desensitises us to a certain degree, that the actions we see played on our television set allow us to build an immunity towards it, so much so that acting out those actions does not impact us emotionally, the way that it should. It's a complex issue, one that people will debate about for years, especially after a school shooting like Pembrook.'

'You think there will be more shootings like that?'

'I don't think Pembrook was an isolated incident. I don't think your brother was the one student to have thought it, and he certainly isn't going to be the last. It's a part of our society now. It crept in when we weren't paying attention, and now it's here.'

'So you don't think violent videogames and movies are to blame?'

'No, I think it's much more than that. It has to be. But it's easier sometimes to look to those things, to blame the film companies and the videogaming industries.'

'I visited the town where Robert Hurd lived.'

'Why?'

'To look for answers, I guess. But I didn't find any. Just more questions.' I lowered my head to my chest, and took a deep breath. I could feel my emotions getting away from me.

'Charlie wasn't on drugs,' I finally said.

'I don't believe everything I read in the paper. You should know that by now.'

I nodded. 'He wasn't filled with rage. He didn't hurt animals. He didn't talk about killing people. He didn't keep a journal filled with hate notes and a detailed hit list. And he didn't grow up alone. He grew up with me.'

'What you're talking about is a term we call Typology. It's when we stereotype people who kill and deem them all socially detached, bullied, depressed loners.'

'I feel like I owe you an apology, Dr Albreck. I wasted a lot of your time in the beginning. I can see now that you were only trying to help.'

'You don't need to apologise for anything, Sam. In fact, from where I'm sitting you are apologising too much, and for a lot of things that were and will always be beyond your control.'

'I don't know what else to do, but to say sorry.'

'And that's normal. But you'll learn that apologising for someone else's mistakes will not reverse their actions, or bring that person back.'

'I just keep thinking, what did I miss? But every time I replay the last year or so of Charlie's life, I don't see someone who was plotting a shooting rampage. I don't see a killer. I just see my brother. I see someone who loved to paint, who took photos of his classmates for the yearbook, who beat me every time at Super Mario Brothers. I see someone who took care of me when I had the flu, who made me peanut butter and strawberry jam sandwiches after school, who stuck glow-in-the-dark stickers all over my ceiling so I could pretend that I was in space, staring at the solar system. And now ... now ...' I clenched my jaw, feeling it ache and stiffen.

'You wonder if you ever really knew him at all.' And just like that, she read my mind. She exposed my darkest deepest thought – the kind of thought that eats away at a person, until nothing is left.

A sharp pain filled my chest, and all of a sudden I couldn't breathe. I tried to swallow, but my throat burned. I curled my fists into a ball and covered my face with them. I felt my back shaking and tightening before I realised that I was crying. I tipped my head back, and leaned it on the top of the armchair. Taking a deep breath, I felt such an overwhelming release that I gasped loudly.

Dr Albreck didn't touch me or hand me the box of tissues that sat on the coffee table between us. She didn't give me a patronising nod of sympathy or a false sense of empathy. She just nodded. And I knew that she knew that I had reached that turning point. That was the last time I cried in her office. But it wasn't the last time I saw her. Our sessions became more frequent, the honesty and trust developing with every conversation. She didn't lie to me. She didn't sugar-coat things to make them go down more easily. She didn't have all the answers. But she slowly and gradually helped me to find my own.

Chapter 23

'Heroes' *(Oasis, B-Side, Summer 1997)*

I stared into the mirror at the image that wasn't me. It was of a boy dressed in his brother's black tuxedo that was obviously too big for him. It was of a boy who didn't look like a boy any more. The eyes staring back were those of someone who understood grief, loss and heartbreak. Those eyes were dark and empty, and belonged to a teenager who'd had his adolescence ripped away.

The white shirt itched at my neck and I squirmed in the suit, feeling it hang awkwardly on my thin frame. I longingly looked over at the dark-wash jeans that lay on the floor.

'Leave it on.'

I looked up and saw my dad in the doorway, leaning against the doorframe. 'Leave it on. It suits you better than it suited me. Besides, it's your end-of-year formal. All the other kids will be wearing suits and tuxes.'

'I don't know. I look stupid. It doesn't fit right. And I couldn't figure out the bow tie,' I said, roughly pulling at the collar before throwing my hands up in defeat.

'Here, let me try,' my dad said, as he walked over. He paused when he reached me, but began effortlessly lopping the delicate black satin fabric through his large calloused fingers. 'There.'

I turned back to the mirror and found a symmetrical bow tucked gently under my chin, neatly below the collar. 'Wow. Looks good.'

'Yeah, I'm surprised too,' he laughed. 'Your mum always did mine.' The smile faded fast from his face as his body slumped heavily to the bed. 'I really made a mess of things didn't I, son?'

'No, Dad. This isn't your fault,' I said, sitting beside him on the bed. I felt the tuxedo trousers crease beneath me and knew I was making little lines up the back of my legs. I didn't care.

'I was so hard on you boys. I only ever wanted you two to grow up and be strong. I never wanted this to happen.' He buried his face in his hands and did something I never thought he'd do – he broke. Right in front of me. First, his body trembled then he started to cry softly. But then his back started shaking harder and his cries got louder, more pained and tortured. 'I'm so ashamed of myself.'

'Dad, stop. You can't blame yourself. I learned

that these past few months. I wondered what I did, what I could have done. Maybe if he'd opened up to me, I would have known he was hurting inside. I thought about that every night since last summer. But I realised there was nothing we could have done. And torturing ourselves every day isn't going to bring him back, or those that died in that school. We can't change the past. We can only learn from it.'

'That sounds so grown up,' he said, raising his head up to me, exposing a slight smirk.

'I can't take credit. I stole that line from Dr Albreck,' I grinned.

He laughed gently then rubbed his chin, his fingers grazing the stubble that was beginning to resemble a beard. 'I'm sorry we made you go there.'

'Don't be. She actually really helped me through this. I'm hoping to keep seeing her, for now anyway?'

'Of course. Take as long as you need with her.'

'You know, she's talked about all of us attending a session together. You know, like family counselling? I know you think therapy is stupid, but if we got Mum to go too then it might be good for us.'

'I think that's a great idea, Sam,' he said, wrapping his arm around me. 'What a year. Who would have thought we would have survived this?'

'Not me.'

'Certainly not me. Your mum knew though. She always does.'

'She'll come back, Dad. She's been blaming herself too. But she'll come back, and we'll figure things out.'

'I never did say congratulations for the Music Academy.'

'Who told you?'

'Your mother.' He sighed, his breath hitching at the end. He shook his head and looked at me. 'Sam, I am so proud of you.'

'We'll get through this, Dad,' I said, gingerly resting a hand on his shoulder. Affection was new to us both but I hoped it would soon feel natural, comfortable, less foreign. He reached up and patted my hand, gently nodding his head. I didn't know if he believed me or not, but I did. We had fallen hard, and there was no lower ground to reach. We were at it. And now there was only one direction we could go – up.

***

The collar of my shirt closed in tighter around my neck as I walked up the plush carpeted stairs of the Garden Hotel. Soft music greeted me at the top, the floor beneath my dress shoes slightly vibrating with the heavy bass. Past the arched doorway, beside the lifts, sat two teachers I recognised from school but I didn't quite remember their names. Ms Chester? Or was it Ms Chalmers?

'Welcome to the end-of-year formal,' said the one whose name I faintly knew. As I got closer to the table she sat at, I saw that the nametag on her polka-dot blouse read 'Ms Chalkert – Teacher Chaperone'. When she smiled, it was fake and a pearly pink lipstick stain smudged across her top teeth. 'You can sign the keepsake yearbook here and get your photos over there by the entrance when your date arrives.'

'Actually I'm not waiting for anyone. I'm here alone.'

'Oh. Well, you can head straight in … or if you want, you can have a solo photo?'

A solo photo. No thanks. 'I'll just sign the yearbook and head in.' But when I stood over the yearbook, silver pen in hand, I didn't know what to write. I hadn't any friends to shout out, any memories to document or any words of wisdom to express to younger generations. I had no legacy to leave behind. My footprints in the sand would be quickly washed over by a gentle tide, and I would be forgotten. My brother, however, would not be. But he wasn't me. And I was ready to move forward with my future, even if that meant leaving him and the boy I used to be behind. So, I dropped the pen by the book, untouched by my words, and walked into the hall.

Silver streamers hung vertically from the ceiling, hitting and tickling my face when I entered. Glossy gold balloons littered the wooden floor, with 1997 freestanding flags adorning the white-linen tables. This didn't look like a graduation formal. It reminded me of my cousin Violet's wedding in 1993, even down to the tacky decorations.

The tables were mostly empty, groups scattered across the hall. The eighteen-year-olds and those with fake ID propped themselves up at the bar, already one too many vodka and oranges in. A group of girls from 'Group A' huddled in the corner consoling one of their own as she loudly cried into a linen napkin, likely after being dumped by one of the guys standing around the dance floor swigging beers. Larger clusters had gathered near them and were jumping up and down to 'Barbie Girl' by Aqua. But my eyes were on the beautiful brunette in beige-and-blush tulle in the middle of the dance floor. Hair already growing out, wisps of her locks swayed across her face like a pendulum as she shifted side to side with the music.

'Doesn't she look beautiful?'

I turned around and saw Debbie approaching me from the left, her slight swagger indicating a trip or two to the bar. While most of the sixth-year female population wore long silk dresses, much too low in the front, Debbie had paired a crisp white Hendrix T-shirt with a black net skirt and high-top Converse. She looked like an extra from the Aqua music video, although I doubt she would've taken that as a compliment had I told her.

'Yeah, she does,' I said instead, turning back to Izzy on the dance floor.

'For what it's worth, Sam, I really respect you for how you handled yourself this year. If it had been me, I would have jumped off a bridge or something,' she laughed, then blushed bright red. 'You came to school every morning knowing that people hated you and your family. You tried, every day, when no one expected you to. And you held your own against Dougie, which is no small feat in itself. Good for you, Sam. And congratulations on London, you really deserve it.'

'Thanks, Debbie. That really means a lot.'

'It's been crazy knowing you, Sam, and that's a compliment,' she smiled. 'And here's my end-of-year gift to you.' She turned me and stared me directly in the eyes, her head slightly bobbing to the side. 'Izzy is crazy about you. And has been for a while, I think. Don't let things end like this, especially before they even began.'

Blinking heavily, I stared at Debbie for a moment before words formed on my lips. 'OK,' I simply said, still staring at her. Before she walked away, she gently gripped my arm like my aunt used to when she came to visit us. Those visits were gone now. No one wants to be related to the family who made headlines all throughout 1996 for the wrong reasons – the very wrong reasons.

Heart pounding, I turned back towards Izzy. She had stopped dancing now, and was staring back at me. Hand rising up slowly by my side, I began waving hello when a large bang broke our attention from each other. A wooden chair lay over on its side, spilling out into the dance floor. Lying beside it was Dougie. Clambering to his feet, he suddenly launched himself at Noel who I hadn't noticed had been standing in front of him. At first, I thought they were dancing together then I realised that they were fighting. Limbs crossing over each other, fists in the air, legs trying to coil round the other's to force a trip, their scuffle had everyone gripped. Even Izzy.

Breaking away from the cluster of students she had been dancing near, she ran towards the fight, screaming Dougie's name. Before I had a chance to weigh the better option, I began running too except I was yelling her name, not Dougie's.

When I reached them, more chairs were strewn across the floor and a bigger crowd had formed around them, chanting them to carry on. As I reached out to grab Izzy by the arm, to pull her away from the swelling crowd, Dougie's face caught my eye. Dark-red blood trickled down from his nose, and his left eye was red and puffy. Noel had a split lip but was still spewing out words of anger, hatred. 'Just admit it! You got together with my girlfriend at Andy's party!'

'I didn't touch your girlfriend! Why would I? I can do better than that,' laughed Dougie, as he turned away.

Noel grabbed a beer bottle from the table, and smashed it against the edge of the chair. He held it towards Dougie. 'What did you say?'

'Sam!' I heard Izzy's voice before I noticed what I had done. I had placed myself directly in front of the broken bottle, between Dougie and Noel. I hadn't even felt my feet move, and didn't recall the thought entering my mind. But seeing that sharp glass, that look of blind and vengeful hatred, had taken control of my body.

'What are you doing? Get out of my way, Macmillan.'

'No.' The words poured out as if this conversation had been scripted, previously rehearsed. Perhaps I had replayed a situation like this where I had talked Charlie out of the June shootings. Although that situation ended the same way every time, no matter what words of persuasion and pleading I had provided, this situation would end differently. I didn't care if it was the last thing I ever did, I didn't even care if Noel stabbed me with the cheap beer bottle. All I cared about was changing the outcome of this conversation.

'Sam, you're going to get hurt. Stay out of this. I have it covered,' said Dougie, as he pulled at my arm.

'He looks like he's going to stab you. I don't think you have this covered.' I tore my arm out of his grip and replanted my feet firmly in front of him. 'Noel, put the bottle down.'

'Get out of my way!' he said, switching the bottle to his other hand.

'Noel, this is ridiculous. You're just drunk. You're going to wake up tomorrow and realise how petty this fight was.'

'I'm warning you –'

'– Or what? You're going to stab me? Stab Dougie? You want to be like my brother?'

Noel flinched at the memory of my brother, and a couple of girls started crying as if on a timed cue. 'I'm nothing like your brother!' he laughed manically.

'Really? Because look at yourself – you're standing amongst a group of students with a bottle in your hand and making threats. You look like Charlie to me, and probably to everyone else

here. Look at their faces, Noel. They're scared of
you, scared of what you'll do if provoked. I know
that look. I recognise that look. Hey, I still get
it sometimes. But is that what you want? If you
stab him with that thing, you'll be in the papers
tomorrow. You'll be another depressed teenager
who wanted to hurt people. Because that's what
they'll say you are, regardless of who you are.
Depressed, suicidal, detached, anxious, unable
to make relationships, even with family.' The
words stung my lips like scalding hot water. 'The
papers will ignore the fact that you were one of
the brightest kids in the class, that you loved art
classes, and that you were best friends with your
brother and cared deeply about him. People don't
want to read about that. They want to hear the
good parts – the parts about you that they can
easily relate to a killer – cold, a loner, enjoyed too
many violent video-games. That's what people
want to read. That's what sells the stories. Are you
depressed, Noel? A loner? Suicidal? Do you like to
watch horror movies and play videogames at the
weekends? Are you a killer, Noel? Are you?'

The bottle dropped heavily to the wooden floor.
'I am nothing like your brother, Macmillan,' he spat
at me. Before I could respond, I felt his fist connect
with my face with such a force that it knocked me
off my feet. He was long gone before the police

arrived. And when questioned, students remained quiet. No one quite knew what to say, and how to respond. Noel wasn't a violent boy. He was just pissed off and didn't know how to handle it. Noel hadn't let us down; we'd let him down.

The police finally left, taking the formal dance with them. Clusters broke up into smaller groups and began calling parents and taxis to come take them home. Soon, the hall was empty bar some gold balloons and fallen paper streamers. Stepping over the confetti, I found Izzy sitting at the bottom of the stairs in the lobby.

'How's your nose?'

'Bleeding. Badly it seems.'

'Thanks for helping Dougie, even if he did steal Noel's girlfriend.'

'No problem, I was looking to get a beating on this night. Isn't that how all school formals end?'

She nudged me slightly. 'Well, that was one memorable evening for sure.' She intertwined her hand with mine, our fingers weaving together. 'That was amazing what you did, Sam. That took a lot of courage and honesty.'

'I couldn't just stand there and watch that happen. Not again.'

'Sam, you didn't just stand there. I know you enough now to see that you would have done everything in your power to help those you love.

You couldn't help Charlie. You should never blame yourself. We can't go back in time, so all we can do is move forward. You have so much to look forward to. I am so happy about your acceptance to London.'

'How does everyone seem to know about that? I only just got the acceptance letter.'

'It was in the paper.'

'Of course it was,' I said, shaking my head.

'No, I mean the local evening paper posted an outline of every graduating student's future plans. They do it every year in Knightsbridge.'

I laughed, and realised how crazy I must have looked. 'I actually made the paper for something not related to my brother?'

She nodded, and smiled. 'Are you excited?'

'Yeah,' I said, shaking my head. 'It just seems so far away right now. But I'm looking forward to a new Sam in a new city surrounded by new people.'

'I quite like the old Sam,' she smiled. 'But I'm looking forward to watching you perform at the Royal Academy.'

'Will you come visit me?' I asked, perhaps too eagerly.

'Well, I won't really need to visit you, not now that I've got a place at the University of London right near you,' she said, the corners of her lips turning up as she turned to see my expression.

'You're going to London? That's amazing! Wow, the rebellious Izzy heading to university to study and make her parents proud,' I laughed.

'I realised university was something that I wanted for myself, and not doing it to spite my dad and Carol was actually hurting me not them. So, I applied and I'm officially studying philosophy in September.'

'Congratulations. Although I pity the students who have to debate philosophy with you.'

'I think next year is going to be the best year of our lives,' she smiled, leaning into me. Gently she kissed me on the cheek and gripped my hand tighter. 'Do you like my dress?'

I shrugged. 'Do *you* like your dress? Because that's all that really matters.'

She smiled and fluffed the tulle around her ankles so it would stick out more. 'Yeah, I do. I really do.'

'Then I like it too,' I answered, pressing the napkin harder into my face to stop the blood dripping any further onto my dad's tux.

'Sam, can I ask you something?'

'Sure.'

'Why do you like me so much?'

I shook my head and looked into her eyes, feeling the warmth grow in my cheeks. 'I hope one day you'll realise how amazing you are and how you don't need to change one bit for anyone. You're perfect, Izzy.' My cheeks burned hotter, and I bit down on my lower lip tasting the blood that had already dried there.

Izzy wrapped one arm around me and looked dead straight into my eyes. 'No, Sam. You're the amazing one,' she smiled.

Before I could answer, her lips were on mine. As I awkwardly tried to elevate my head to avoid smearing a blood-soaked rag on her face, it suddenly hit me that I was at my end-of-year formal, kissing the girl of my dreams. I was finally a regular teenager.

When she pulled away, I felt the corners of my mouth turning up into a smug grin. She laughed, then lifted my arm up over her and snuggled into my chest.

'OK, OK, that's enough, Lovebirds.' Dougie staggered out of the boys' bathroom still holding a beer bottle in his hand. Taking a swig from it, he leaned against the railing. 'Sam, forgive me. I've been a total idiot. I didn't deserve Izzy and I stopped you, even though I knew how much you both liked each other. I was a selfish prat.'

'Yes, you were. But I also shouldn't have made my feelings so known while you were both in a relationship so I'm sorry too.' I offered my hand and he shook it firmly, smiling.

Getting up, we all headed towards the front

entrance, linking arms like the school kids we were for the next few hours. Tomorrow we'd be graduated, and the future would be a scary but exciting path for all of us.

'You know,' Dougie said to Izzy, 'I never did get a dance tonight.'

'Yeah, me neither,' I added.

'But there's no music,' she said.

'Follow me,' he said, leading Izzy and me back into the dance hall. He marched over to the big music system and slid his hand into his suit jacket. Surfacing beneath the black fabric was a silver disc covered in black marker doodles.

'You carry a music CD with you?' I laughed.

'You never know when a party's going to need some livening up,' he winked, sliding the CD into the plastic tray and pushing it in gently. The tray sucked the disc inside and a faint amber glow twinkled across several buttons. 'Let's see ... perfect, just the song for our last dance as teenagers.'

A burst of crackling seeped in through the loudspeakers, and quickly turned into the Clash's 'Rock the Casbah'. Izzy threw her arms up in the air and howled. Dougie broke out into a dance, his limbs effortlessly moving in perfect rhythm. As the cleaners mopped the floors around us and the barmen collected half-empty glasses from the tables, the three of us danced together the first and last time at our graduation formal. Izzy's tulle bounced around as she twirled, and a smile stretched wide across her face when her eyes met mine. The moment was perfect. We were perfect.

After, Dougie collected the CD and handed it to me. I slipped it inside my jacket, and led the way to the hotel doors. Stepping into the cold air, we all took a deep breath. 'Wow, the stars are so bright tonight,' said Izzy, pointing up towards the sky.

We trotted down the driveway, and looped past the hotel gates. Pembroke was over fifteen miles away from here, but I didn't feel like calling my dad or hailing a taxi. I wanted to walk beside Izzy and Dougie for as long as I could. I didn't want this moment to end.

The breeze gently whipped at our faces, and somewhere in the distance crickets chirped songs in the night. Small thatched houses stood side by side like a row of soldiers awaiting battle. Faint shimmers of light shone through some windows, while others were in darkness. The odd window hid from us, clouded over like a cataract.

'What's your plans for the future, Dougie?' I asked him.

His feet stumbled over stones and sometimes slipped off the edge of the pavement, the consumption of beers and gin evident. 'Me? I'm not one for universities and further education. I think real learning is accomplished out there, beyond classroom walls.'

As if we could see something concrete, we all looked to where Dougie was gesturing. I guess the real world was beyond the fences and neatly trimmed lawns of village streets. 'What about London?'

'London is on my list,' he said. 'First, I'm taking the train to Paris then Brussels. Amsterdam, Barcelona, Madrid – I'm doing it all. Wherever the Eurostar won't take me, some bus will.'

'You're taking a gap year? For how long?'

'A year, maybe two. That's the best part – I have no plans, no timetable, just me and my camera.'

'Well, we intend to see all your photos when you get back,' said Izzy, linking her arm through his too.

'Definitely,' he smiled, nudging her playfully.

'Promise?' I asked.

'Promise.'

Chapter 24

'Bitter Sweet Symphony' (The Verve, Summer 1997)

Coming together like the violins, cellos and clarinets of Samuel Barber's *Adagio for Strings*, the bittersweet arrival of the scattering of Charlie's ashes was idyllic and dreamlike. The day swept in like a gentle wave at morning tide, and as if we had set an alarm we all awoke at the same time. Quietly gathering our clothes, we dressed and ate breakfast in silence. Mum had returned the night before, choosing to sleep in the spare bedroom. The love that had faded and turned to resentment would never return, but in its place a friendship would grow.

Ascending and descending like an arch, the composition of the song I heard in my head turned everything around into a slowed-down tempo. Each step my parents took consumed time, their feet gently and gradually touching the ground before rising up again. Even the birds in the sky flapped their wings at such a slow pulse.

As the musical arrangement in my mind intensified towards a climactic end, we reached the edge of the cliff. Harper's Beach was the perfect spot to finally let my brother's ashes go. We had held onto these remains with the same ferocity as we had held onto the emotions and painful memories of last summer. We weren't ready to let go of Charlie until recently. And although I had thought about doing it myself all these months as I watched Mum and Dad blame each other and those all around them, I was relieved to not have done so. It wouldn't have been right, or fair to my brother, to release his ashes into the wind while still harbouring the same feelings that had almost drowned me and destroyed our family. Only now were we free of my brother's ghost, and the ghosts of every life he had taken that day.

We would never know what he was thinking that morning, and why he did it. Like the police, the media and the victims' families, we could only speculate and theorise. The blame would never fully leave us nor release us from its tight grasp, but the weight of our loss and guilt was easing with every passing day.

'Are you ready?' said Mum, as she looked between Dad and me.

Soft tears trickled down my dad's cheeks as he gently nodded. 'You should do it, Sam. Charlie would have wanted that.'

Mum handed me the small clay pot. It was lighter than I had imagined. All those years, all those memories fitted into one small jar. I held it up towards the vibrant sun, feeling the brightness sting my eyes slightly.

'Goodbye, Brother. I hope you knew how loved you were. You will be missed more than you will ever know.'

Amidst the hysterical sobbing of my mother beside me, a crisp silence surrounded us like a dense mist. I could hear no seagulls, no lapping of waves, just the breathing of the air into our lungs. I slid the lid off the pot and gently tipped it over the edge. Particles of a dark dust poured out smoothly, riding the breeze for a while before settling into its home in the ocean. When the pot was empty, I placed the lid back on and handed it to my dad to bury when we got home. To fill the inside, I had ripped out several pages of my journal to bury with it, including my last entry:

Dear Charlie,

This will be the last time I write in this book, on these pages. The first time I wrote to you, I was angry with you. I was so angry with you. I thought you were selfish, and now I realise that I was the selfish one. I was so preoccupied by what I was feeling, what I was going through, that I didn't stop to think about what you were going through.

I will never know what happened that day in June. I will never know what went through your mind when you walked into that school, what your final thought was when you pulled the trigger, or whether you considered me, or Mum or Dad in any of this. And I have to be OK with that. I have to believe that you thought about us, that you loved us. And I'm starting to, I really am.

I've changed. And I can't tell you enough how amazing that feels. It's still hard, but I don't think that ever goes away. But it gets a little easier every day. And that's what I have to concentrate on - the little moments, the days, not the future. Because I don't know what the future will bring. All I know for certain is that you will always be with me.

Charlie, there's not one day that I don't think about you, that I don't miss you. You were my big brother and I looked up to you. I will treasure the memories of us playing Connect 4 on camping trips, creating scenarios where you were Sherlock Holmes and I was Dr Watson, riding our bikes down the trails, playing Jaws *in the swimming pool, holding ice cream eating competitions in the kitchen. The memories I have of us growing up together will be the best memories of my life. You were always so kind and caring to me, and I wish we had been able to show the world that. They see what they want to see, and that's OK because I see you, the real you. I love you, Charlie. You are finally at peace.*

I folded the final page and placed it so delicately inside the urn, as if it would break. As if my words would shatter it. But I knew it was stronger than that. I knew *I* was stronger than that.

And there it was. My deepest thoughts would be buried alongside the vessel that had protected my brother all those months. My words would fill the emptiness inside, fill the void within.

And as I walked back towards the car, hearing the final notes of *Adagio for Strings*, I looked back and saw my father embracing my mother. He cradled her head gently as she sobbed into his chest. Tears trickled down his cheek as he held her tighter. And it was then that I realised, we would be OK.

Amnesty International UK endorses this book because it reminds us that human rights belong to all of us.

The Universal Declaration of Human Rights (UDHR) was signed in 1948 by world leaders who wanted to prevent horrors like the Holocaust from ever happening again. It sets out thirty rights, or freedoms, that protect all of us, whoever we are and wherever we live. Amnesty International is a movement of ordinary people from across the world standing up for humanity and human rights. Our purpose is to protect individuals wherever justice, fairness, freedom and truth are denied. You can join us to stand up and show solidarity for our rights, for other people and for ourselves.

> *All human beings are born free and equal in dignity and rights.'*
> Article 1, UDHR.

Dear Charlie shows how challenging it can be to respect the universality of human rights. N.D. Gomes doesn't just encourage us to feel empathy for Sam, she pushes us to think about Charlie too. While we don't get answers as to why someone is driven to kill, she pushes us to think beyond the headlines and not to dehumanise someone who has committed an inhuman act. Applying human rights to people who scare or horrify us can be very difficult, but it is fundamental to ensuring we are all offered justice, dignity, equality and freedom.

If you want to stand up for human rights, you can:
- find out how to start a Youth Group in your school or community www.amnesty.org.uk/youth
- the Junior Urgent Action network: www.amnesty.org.uk/jua
- Take action online for individuals at risk around the world: www.amnesty.org.uk/actions

If you are a teacher or librarian, you are welcome to use our many free resources for schools at www.amnesty.org.uk/education

Amnesty International UK,
The Human Rights Action Centre, 17-15 New Inn Yard, London EC2A 3EA
Tel: 020 7033 1500
Email: sct@amnesty.org.uk